dear stupid penpal

rascal hartley

Cover art by Carly A-F
Interior Illustrations by Matt Blairstone
Edited by Alex Woodroe

Published by Tenebrous Press.
Visit our website at www.tenebrouspress.com.

First Printing, November 2025.

Print ISBN: 978-1-959790-43-3
eBook ISBN: 978-1-959790-44-0

Cover art by Carly A-F.

Interior illustrations by Matt Blairstone.

Edited by Alex Woodroe.

Formatting by Lori Michelle Booth.

All creators in this publication have signed an AI-free agreement. To the best of our knowledge, this publication is free from machine-generated content.

Selected Works from Tenebrous Press:

Clairviolence: Tales of Tarot and Torment
stories by Mo Moshaty

Reef Life
a novella by Hazel Zorn

Puppet's Banquet
a novella by Valkyrie Loughcrewe

Casual
a novel by Koji A. Dae

All Your Friends are Here
stories by M.Shaw

TRVE CVLT
a novel by Michael Bettendorf

A Spectre is Haunting Greentree
a novel by Carson Winter

From the Belly
a novel by Emmett Nahil

Mouth
a novella by Joshua Hull

Lumberjack
a novella by Anthony Engebretson

Posthaste Manor
a novel by Jolie Toomajan & Carson Winter

The Black Lord
a novella by Colin Hinckley

Dehiscent
a novella by Ashley Deng

More titles at www.TenebrousPress.com

For Mia
May we always see the same stars.

Sorry. I don't think you're stupid, but I'm not in the habit of backspacing and I don't intend to start now. This whole *thing* is stupid, though. Space was cool for all of one day before it became a pain in my ass. And we haven't even hit hyperspeed yet.

Tolstoy says the penpal thing is important—something about "maintaining our earthen roots" or some shit. I don't know. I don't care. Honestly, I hope you're not a scientist, because I've had all the science talk I can *take*.

Meredith goes on and on about like . . . chemical compounds in food and how they might react to deep space. Swear to God, she could make a *McDouble* sound bad. And Todd is so fucking—He like, carries a caliper around with him. *Constantly*. Just *measuring things*. Did you know my hand is 1.5 inches thick? You wanna guess how I know that?

Mateo is awful, Ashraf is awful, Chloe is awful . . . just assume they're all awful. I'm awful, too, of course. Just a spaceship full of awful people going to do technical work an entire galaxy away. Yay us. I hope they read this. I hope they mutiny me before we make it to the outer arms. Not that I'm captain, but . . . you get the idea.

HA! Tolstoy *was* reading this! I just got a message from CC telling me to introduce myself and talk about my hobbies. Hi, Tolstoy. Fuck off.

I'm an astronaut, I'm 28, I like languages. That's why I'm on this godforsaken mission. They needed a *linguist,* in case we wind up stumbling across ET or the Predator, so they offered me the job. And I, being somewhat young, extremely dumb, and horrifically broke, had basically no choice but to agree. But I'm gonna complain the entire time, I *assure you*.

Bleh. Tolstoy is saying I need to comm in to talk about my "emotional aggression" so I guess I'm gonna hit send before he can stop me, byeeeeee.

Dear Unnamed Patron,

Hello! It is nice to hear from you. I'm glad you are doing—if not well—at least okay. It sounds like you're having a rough time.

I know you said you are beginning to loathe space, and I find that unfortunate. I would adore being in space, I think, but it's not meant to be. When it stops irking you so, I might insist you describe it to me.

You said you like languages? Fascinating! I, too, am a purveyor of sorts. Mostly old, ancient languages, and a sprinkling of colloquialisms. They change so rapidly, languages. Even now, people are using words I don't know, or else no longer know in this new context. I think that's why I like the old ones; no one is using Latin to make new words for phalluses.

I shall also take Tolstoy's advice. I'm assuming he will be reading mine, as well, so hello, Tolstoy. It is a pleasure to make your acquaintance.

My name is Aku, I am 29 years old, and I think my favorite hobbies are stargazing and flying. I live alone, mostly. My friends are all off living their own lives, but they stop by sometimes. Alexandria might as well be my sister, for how long we have known each other. She is coming by tomorrow to stay for a while.

Oh, I like to travel, as well. I've been almost everywhere you can think of. Ask me anything. I could tell you of ancient Rome. Or modern Rome, but that's not as cool.

Yours,
Aku

Aku:

Up until that last bit I legit thought I was talking to someone's grandpa. Lighten up your words some, bud. Type how you talk.

Describe space?? Geez, it's dark and there are stars and it's cold and there is not a single Taco Bell.

Do you speak many other languages? Which are your favorites? What did you grow up speaking? What made you interested in languages? Literally no one else here cares about them. I'm dying of linguistic thirst.

Re: Flying? Like in an airplane?

Re: Stargazing: I'm waving, can you see me? (That's a joke; only the Webb could see us now)

Re: Travel: the way you phrased that makes it sound like you were in ancient Rome. How were the gladiator fights, my guy? (Guy?)

Alexandria must be nice, to stick by you so long. Tell her I said hi, and have fun spending time with her.

(How was that, Tolstoy? Nice enough this time?)

—Finch

Dear Finch,

Finch. What a fascinating name! Like the bird, I presume. Also: yes, guy. I should ask if you are a "guy" as well, I suppose. It doesn't really matter to me, but Alexandria is insisting. She says hello back.

Excellent description of space. I am rebutting with my own description of the gladiator fights: geez, they were bloody and cramped and sweltering, and there was not a single Taco Bell.

I do speak many languages, yes. A rather ridiculous amount, I'm told. I grew up speaking Akkadian, but I rarely have opportunity to use that anymore. I'm sure most of it has fled my brain by now. I do not have a favorite language. They are all beautiful in their own way.

Flying: Sure. Like in an airplane.

Stargazing: I see many twinkling lights, and I assume one of them must be you. Hello, up there. I hope things are going better. I'll be staring your way all night, hoping for a glimpse.

This feels disjointed. Does it feel disjointed to you?

Hello, Tolstoy. Goodbye, Tolstoy.

Yours,
Aku

Aku,

Yeah, it does feel disjointed. Let me see if I can work this all into something resembling a single message and not ten in a trench coat:

Okay, so, my name isn't *really* Finch. It's Atticus, but everyone insists on calling me Finch. Always have. So, call me Finch. I'm a guy, too. I wonder if that was just luck of the draw, or if it was intentional, to pair us up like this. I've talked to my crewmates a bit more now, and they're not *quite* as awful as I initially thought. I could probably ask them about their penpals, too. In fact, I will. Hold on.

Okay, it was just luck of the draw. Lucky us, two linguists locked in literary letters. :)

We all have our own penpals, and everyone seems to be liking the program so far. It's good for us to talk about things that *aren't* space-related. Aku, I am so tired of space already. It's beautiful. It's endless. If I use the telescope mounted on our ship, I can see the bright colors of distant galaxies. I can still see Earth, too, if I point it that way. It sort of tends to stay pointed that way. I think everyone might be a little afraid of the arrival of the day where we can no longer see home.

We have to get far enough away from Earth to engage hyperdrive, so that's what we're all waiting around for. We're not in deep space yet, but based on the decreasing size of Earth, we will be soon. Sometimes I turn the telescope in the direction we're going, and all I see are star clusters light years away. You asked for a description of space, so here it is: lonely. Space is undeniably lonely. The stars don't twinkle because there is no atmosphere to make them do so; they just stare right back at you and beckon you closer, and no matter how close you get, they're still just as far away. If I look too long, I feel terror in my heart. That is space. Was that good enough to get a better description of Rome?

I wanted to go to Rome. I wanted to go a lot of places. We'll eventually return home, you know, but what if something catastrophic happens? What if we drift into space forever and I die out here? Do I decompose once the airlocks fail? I'd ask Meredith, but honestly, I'm afraid of the answer. Tell me about Rome? Please?

Geez, sorry. I'd backspace all that, but I don't do that, so . . . enjoy the mini existential crisis, bud.

Um . . . so, Akkadian, that's funny! Akkadian was on my list of dead languages to do a deeper dive into. I've gotta convince Tolstoy to steal some materials from restricted libraries for me. Pretty please, Tolstoy? Look how nice I'm being! This niceness could be all yours for the low low price of petty theft!

Or, you know, if *you* could teach me some Akkadian (if you really do know some), I'd love you forever or whatever. I'll take the Sharpie I definitely didn't smuggle onboard and write your name on the walls of this ship. Wait, Tolstoy can't reach me now. I totally smuggled a Sharpie onboard.

Heh, he sent me a message telling me to put it in a hazardous waste bag and let it exit the ship. No way, José, this baby is alllll miiiiiine.

Speaking of loving you forever or whatever, my guy, you can't just *say shit* like "I'll be staring your way all night, hoping for a glimpse." That's some Brontë shit right there. Oh, do you write anything? What's your favorite book? I feel like I'd love to read something by you. Sorry for when I said you write like a grandpa, I didn't mean it in a bad way. Sort of a classics way. You know what I mean.

Anyway, how was your time with Alexandria? What did you guys do? Also: if you're insinuating you have a pilot's license, I'm going to need you to promise to fly me somewhere cool when I get done with this mission. Maybe Rome.

—Finch

Dear Finch,

I'll keep the Brontë-isms to a minimum. For now. I can spare a few Akkadian words though: kakkabu, meaning stars. Shamash, the sun. Sin, the moon. Most of those are the names of old gods, but they'll work fine. Let's test them out:

I look up to the kakkabu tonight, hoping to see your spaceship, yet knowing I won't. You are far past Sin, and heading, I'm assuming, in a direction opposite Shamash. Tell Ishtar (Venus) I said hello. It has been long since I've met with her. (Yes, I know she is opposite you, but you are both in space, and I am not.) Do you know Akkadian mythology? I'll tell you: the sun is the child of the moon. I once thought it should be reversed, but looking up at the moon tonight, it feels correct.

I told Alexandria, when we sat together, reading your letter, that you were up there, in the cosmos. She still finds it hard to believe we've advanced enough to send people there. She bought a telescope and we sat for hours, debating where you might be, if our telescope was giant and not some rickety thing on three legs. Where are you? Where should I look to pretend to see you?

Space is dark. I noticed that as we gazed through the lens. We at least had the noises and lights of the city surrounding us; I cannot imagine being fully encompassed. It sounds like when I once sailed through endless ocean, the way it looked at night, like you would never get home, because the dark was vast and infinite. I'm sorry. Know that I am scanning every inch of sky, so, statistically, I am looking at you, somewhere.

To give you something new to imagine: Rome.

Rome was always warm, a pleasant sort of feeling. Like the world was always caring for you, specifically, making sure you did not encounter terrible things. Which, of course, was ironic, for how terrible it truly was. For the time, it was splendid, but looking back gives you all sorts of new insights. The gladiator duels being one of them, of course. They were coarse and bloody, but the crowd cheered so loudly and so intensely that it was futile to resist the excitement. We watched people die for the sport of it, and I hate to say it was fun. We can act like we would *never,* that such a thing would *immediately* strike us as morally wrong, but the truth is that it just . . . didn't. It was just something that happened. Men fought to the death for entertainment. So it goes.

Perhaps tell me about your crewmates, now that you know them a bit better? I'd like to know all about them.

Yours,
Aku

Aku:

Do you understand what minimum means, my guy?

I like the way you talk like you were there. And don't think I didn't notice how you avoided my questions about whether you've written anything; I will henceforth be browsing my digital library and finding which books match your cadence. Be forewarned, or whatever.

Ugh, my crewmates? They're not friends. They're more like . . . cousins my mom forced me to spend the night with at their birthday sleepover that I was only invited to because we lived down the road. Or maybe that's not a universal experience.

So we've got Meredith Stucco, Todd Trimble, Mateo Hajjar, Ashraf Perez, Chloe Brignac, and yours truly, Finch Davani. Six person mission. Plus Dominic Tolstoy and all the others at Command Central and Mission Control.

Meredith is our chemist, I think? I'm sorry, this is about to be awful because I am awful at science. I'm in charge of translating things and making sure the plants don't die, and I've already been relieved of one of those duties. She's always talking about chemical compounds. I think she's probably funny? She makes these jokes I don't understand and Chloe always laughs, so she's probably funny. I've got a chemistry textbook pulled up so I can understand her fucking jokes. It's driving me crazy. I think if I pretend it's just another new language, I can figure it out. Anyway! Meredith is sweet in her own way. She's a bit stand-off-ish at first, and she's apt to just take something away from you if you're doing it wrong and just do it herself. Independent, actually, might be the word I'm looking for. She's not mean, though. Just impatient.

Todd is . . . Todd. He's buff, man. He's a mechanical engineer, as far as I can tell. He fixes things around the spaceship and is always—yeah, I told you about the caliper thing. He's all about hard data and building. He brought a Lego set onboard and at first I thought he just gets bored easily, but turns out he's some sort of certified Lego Master (which is a thing???) and is working on a new way to make a sphere. I don't get it, but he assures me

dd is... Todd. He's buff, man. He's a ni
as I can tell. He fixes things around t
s—yeah, I told you about the caliper
ata and building. He brought a Lego s
hought he just gets bored easily, bur

it's important and won't let me play with his Legos. So, fuck that guy.

Mateo and Ashraf are kind of the same person, personality-wise. They're inseparable. They went to college together and have been roommates ever since. (I have been attempting to trick them into telling me if they are *more* than roommates, but alas, my efforts have been fruitless.) They're both gentle and kind souls, with quick wits and more inside jokes than a high school cafeteria table. They're always trying to get me to do things with them. It's a bit unnerving. Um, Mateo is the main pilot and Ashraf functions as the co-pilot. Or captain and co-captain, but I'm not giving them that honorific. Mateo is an astrophysicist, but every time I see him taking measurements or running experiments, he just seems more and more frustrated with his findings. So, yeah. Physicist. Ashraf is some sort of biologist and also *our* biologist? Like, he's our medic, which I'm pretty sure he's not actually trained in. If I break an arm trying to steal some Legos, we're fucked.

Chloe is our astronomer, so she's probably the most indispensable member of our crew. She also has a degree in geology, but that's really only useful if we *do* find some alien planet. So maybe she's here for the same reason I am. She's very sweet, but also will not hesitate to punch you. Which I know because she did not hesitate to punch me when I thought it'd be funny to jump out and surprise her. Fun fact: in space, a punch sends you slo-mo-ing back until you hit a wall. She mostly sticks with Meredith now. They've become fast friends, and I'm totally not jealous at all. (Of the friend thing.) She's teaching Meredith French, and I've mentioned that I speak French already, but she mostly uses that information to tell me what to do. In French. I don't know; Chloe is hard to work out.

And then you've got me, Finch. Er, I'm the linguist, you already know. I think I'm also some sort of peacemaker here. I didn't know that going in, but when we had my "emotional aggression" meeting, Tolstoy kept going on and on about how it was important that I maintained a level head. Apparently that's one of the reasons they picked me: because I can handle myself in a crisis. I am Crisis Captain. If Ashraf and Mateo suddenly go into panic mode, I'm in charge. Which is, really, a horrible decision. I don't even get the chemistry jokes, and I don't consider myself any sort of "peacemaker". Um, I'm stand-off-ish. I don't mean to be. I like talking, but no one here likes what I want to talk about, so I just . . . don't. I think they think I'm quiet and shy. I'm not. I just don't know what to say, and to be fair, they're not exactly making an effort, either. But I've got a few textbooks downloaded, so maybe we can meet in the middle. Ugh. If I come out of this a scientist, I'm blaming Tolstoy.

Tolstoy is our communications guy, by the way. He vets messages going in and out. Hi, Tolstoy. He's reading this now. Poor guy. He's like our IT man, and I bet the others don't even realize he can see all the porn they probably download. Does our ship have viruses, Tolstoy? It would be a little funny if it did.

Yeah, he's not answering, ha.

It's getting harder to see Earth in the telescope. I bet we looked at each other last night. Do you wait until night to respond to me on purpose? Do you just sit outside and look up and talk to me? Backspace backspace backspace. Ugh. Maybe I'm kind of lonely. There are lots of kakkabu out. And so Venus is Ishtar, huh? You're closer to her than me, but I'll tell her hi. Was there a word for Jupiter? Should I be making some sort of offering to Ishtar when I tell her hello from the heavens? I'm dying to have a reason to steal some Legos, and if I cite religious reasons, I don't think Todd can do anything about it.

So, Sin bore Shamash, huh? It makes sense to me. I know the sun is older, but the moon just has this aura about it. It feels more absolute, somehow. I always liked the moon.

I don't have anything else to say, really, other than thanks. For talking to me. (Read that as not mushy, please.)

—Finch

PS WAIT YES I DO, YOU WERE A SAILOR?!?!

Dear Finch,

Ah yes, of course. Nothing about you radiates "peacemaker," so I'm not sure why they chose you. (Read that as sarcastic, please.)

Your crew sound like an interesting bunch. Maybe they're in the same boat as you, so to speak. Maybe you're all afraid to stick too far out, so none of you do. Maybe Todd would teach you how to build a Lego sphere, if you asked. I don't know. I'd just hate for you to be stuck up there with people you disliked.

To answer your question: yes, I do wait until night to read your letters, but not intentionally. I tend to wake up closer to nightfall. I do look up and imagine you're speaking them to me. Is that another thing I shouldn't have said? I can't quite tell the difference.

(Am I repeating sentence structures to throw you off my scent? Perhaps!)

You can absolutely steal Legos in the name of Ishtar. I am, in fact, begging you to do so. Make something cool. Maybe a dragon. Make me a dragon, Finch.

Jupiter wasn't a god, for us. The word we used was nibiru, and then only during certain periods of time. Nibiru was also the North Star, and Mercury, and sometimes even Venus herself. See something bright in the night sky? Nibiru.

I wish I had something long to talk about. What would you like to hear? Could I have a day's log of your mission? I'm so curious what happens up there, but only if Tolstoy allows it. I'll talk with you about anything.

Yours,
Aku

PS Yes, I sailed for a considerable length of time in a rather well-known triangle of ocean.

Aku:

Okay okay holy shit you sailed the *Bermuda Triangle?* Was it cool? Did anything incredible happen? Please write me a novel detailing your adventures. Due by tomorrow. Please and thank you.

In exchange, *I* will write you a novella about my day today, since you asked so nicely. Well, maybe not a novella. A short story, perhaps. Or flash fiction. You get the idea.

We keep our clocks set to Houston time, to make everyone's lives easier. My alarm was set to 6:30 in the morning, and I thoroughly and promptly destroyed it the first time it went off. So now I wake up when I want to. :)

Usually I'd keep the plants alive, but seeing as I am bad at that, Ashraf now keeps the plants alive. Which—*for the record,* these plants hate me in particular. I'm *not* a bad plant parent! I had a whole succulent I kept alive and I *swear* if you say something about how succulents don't die I'll make Tolstoy block you.

You might find yourself wondering just how a linguist with minimal plant experience wound up in charge of plants onboard a super serious space mission. Well, good news, because I'm going to tell you.

Bad news, Tolstoy told me not to tell you.

I don't see *why;* it's not like it's top secret that our original botanist turned out to be a

Motherfucker disabled my keyboard for AN ENTIRE GODDAMN HOUR. We just had to have *another* meeting! This one about what is and is not public information. We really should've had these meetings *before* we left Earth.

Speaking of, I told Ishtar hi for you. I even made the best Lego sphere I could for her, as an idol or something. It was really just four blocks arranged in a weird rectangle but I think she got the message. We're picking up speed now. Should be passing Nibiru soon. We're really far from Earth.

Oh right. My routine. How far did I get, again? Ah. To "waking up." Lovely.

Right so, I wake up when I want to and I do my sanctioned morning exercises, which are way too early, still, and then head to the kitchen to grab breakfast/lunch. Unfortunately, none of us are any form of chef, so it's mostly the rations that got packed. We have stuff for like, macaroni and shit like that but . . . none of us really know how.

(Stop. Stop laughing. If you're laughing. I bet you're laughing.)

Listen last time I tried to make ramen I caught the water on fire, alright? You don't want me near the hotplates.

So after I eat a cereal bar and drink some rehydrated milk (shudder), I start doing my *actual* duties: namely, translating logs and typing up everyone's reports in whichever target language it is that day. Then I start my "important training" where they're really just trying to make me more useful on the ship. Which, fine by me. I don't mind knowing a little engineering if it means I can have my free time back when all is said and done.

After that I just sort of . . . wander. I don't know. There's more downtime on a spaceship than I thought there would be. Or maybe, there just is now. Once we're out of the solar system, we can engage hyperdrive, and then we'll have more to do. Right now it's mostly a waiting game. Tick tock tick tock and all that.

I finished that chemistry textbook and even did the practice tests at the end. I tried to engage Meredith in a chemistry conversation, but I think I went in a bit too confident because she got excited and started mentioning concepts I've never even *heard of.* Le sigh. Guess I'm making Tolstoy find me the next twelve volumes in the series. I also watched some videos about rocks, but they were really, *really* fucking boring. It might be better if I just like . . . ask Chloe to talk about them herself. Ugh. *Conversation.*

(Yes. I see the irony.)

You're different, though. It's easy to talk to you. Maybe because I can empty my brain out and you catch it, and then you empty yours right back and I catch it, too. A full reset on both sides, everything we wanna say, uninterrupted. (Right?) Talking with others is different. They don't feel as . . . patient? Which, I guess you don't really have a *choice* on whether or not you're patient, but it feels like you are. Are you? Do I talk too much? I think sometimes I talk too much. Bleh.

Anyway, Mateo and Ashraf are always trying to talk to me but I don't know, I don't connect with them very well. They're "up at 5 in the morning to go for a jog" type of people and I just cannot relate. I sort of wish I could, since they actually make a little bit of an effort. Maybe I'll wake up early tomorrow. Not a lot. Just a little. Just . . . before noon, or something.

Okay so I kill time and then I sort of read and reread your letters a couple times, just to be sure I address everything the best I can before I start typing my own. I also make sure to go look in the telescope before I send it, so we can do that "eye contact" thing. Boop. I just got up and did it. I don't even know where you live, shit. What if it isn't night there? Am I missing you? I'll become nocturnal, scout's honor. Not like time has any meaning up here, anyway.

So after I harass Tolstoy to see if you've responded yet (even though you always send yours after I fall asleep, or else—damn, I wonder if Tolstoy just doesn't deliver it because he knows we'd be up all night. Let me know.) I go for supper/late night snack. Sometimes I have to avoid everyone else because they're having like . . . team meetings or something. I know I'm not exactly . . . *useful* yet, to the mission, or at least not to the logistics of it, so I understand *why* they meet without me, I just . . .

I don't know how I want to end that. I guess I should end by saying "Goodnight, Aku. Sweet dreams." Is it lame I don't want to say goodnight? Like if I just keep typing I can pretend I'm not in space, barreling away from everything I've ever known.

Ah. Tolstoy is calling another "existential dread" meeting with me. At least I always have you, Tolstoy <3

(He sent a heart back. A true friend.)

It is getting late, and I get weird when it's late. Lucky you, I suppose.

Goodnight, Aku. Sweet dreams.

—Finch.

Dear Finch,

You asked for a novel. I am delivering. (Forgive me for not responding to the rest of your letter just yet; I think you need this much more.)

It is stormy.

That is the first thing you truly notice about the Bermuda Triangle: the storms are otherworldly and haunting. The fog rolls in waves, unlike any fog I have ever known. It almost feels like sand against your skin, sand that covers everything until you're lost in liminality.

I was the sole "passenger" aboard a cargo ship. I was granted a place via much bartering and begging, and I was let on with the caveat that I had to help the cook with nighttime prep. I agreed.

I'm not sure what your experience with sailing is, but being on a ship in choppy waters is like standing up in a rollercoaster.

Gravity stops making sense. I was roused awake by the sheer *noise* of waves breaking against the hull. When I emerged on deck, I thought, for sure, it was the end of me.

Waves as tall as the mast; taller, even. They crashed onto the deck and knocked some crewmembers off. I tried to dive after them, but when I made it to the railing and looked down . . . Finch, there was no ocean. We were beached.

Almost as soon as I noticed that, I noticed the sun.

Suffice it to say, I was shocked. I knew, immediately, that something was wrong, that it was . . . that it was some sort of *illusion,* but I could not figure out what kind.

The crewmembers that had fallen were now on the sand, scrambling to their feet. The rest of the crew followed. I hung back as long as I could, but there was only so much I could do to resist the allure of dry land after so long at sea.

The sand was warm and soft, even as I dripped water onto it. That's the only way I knew the storm wasn't merely a dream: I was soaked from head to toe. The captain immediately began ordering a shelter to be built and food to be found as he took to looking for fresh water. He was always a sturdy, smart one. Captain Teague. I don't think I'll ever forget him.

I aided them in pulling down saplings for a rudimentary shelter, then took to exploring further into the forest. There were bits of metal strewn about, small at first, but steadily larger. I gathered a few for the shelter, then finally looked to the canopies.

I saw something I did not recognize then, but do now: a seaplane.

I climbed up to it and looked around inside, but whoever had crashed there had managed to escape. But, based on the single femur still in the plane, they did not make it far.

I took what I thought would be useful and went back to the beach, where the crew were happily making a fire and roasting a freshly-killed boar. I upgraded the shelter and joined them around the fire. The food smelled wrong. Everything smelled wrong.

They offered me food, and I, curious and suspecting something horrid, accepted. It tasted like food. Yet, it was entirely and wholly off. I can't explain, not even now. It was like food in a dream, half-existing and false.

I tried to convince them to leave, but no one seemed to hear me, not with supposedly-plentiful food and drink, fruit and shelter, fire and fish. It was a paradise, as far as they were concerned, and there was no need to leave. I even told them about the crashed machine I had seen, but they saw nothing ominous about it.

The sun was still in the sky. The taste of food was still on my lips. The hair on the back of my neck was at attention. I had to get out of there.

I took one of the dinghies from the ship and began rowing. No one would come with me. They weren't destined to, I suppose. I stood no chance in the ocean, with no cover from the weather, but whatever the island brought was evil. I was sure of that. Whichever death the sea offered me would be kinder.

I should have died, truly. I watched the island disappear, and as I rowed, the days and nights passed in each breath. A thousand years must have gone by.

I am grateful I had a watch, for I was at the shore of Florida in twenty minutes.

I tried to send a rescue team, and a boat did go out, but there was no island they could find for miles. It had disappeared, crew and all. I never saw any of them again.

That is my Bermuda Triangle story. I hope it was everything you desired. Next time, I'll respond to your letter better.

Yours,
Aku

PS I live in New York. We are looking at each other.

Sorry. Fuck. Give me a moment.

Okay. Shit.

Um, right.

Aku:

I'm glad we're staring at each other. I'm tired of being alone.

The BERMUDA fucking TRIANGLE, MAN. I don't even care if it was all made up like . . . that's insane and I love it. Also now I have a piece of your writing to parse. Mwahaha.

I'll toss the ball back into your court but wow, imagining that really happening and not some sort of mirage . . . pfblowww. That's the sound of my brain exploding. Honestly, thank you. I did need that. How'd you pin me down so quickly, huh? Does my shadowbox at least look nice? Tell me about your day. Tell me about your childhood. Whatever you wanna say.

—Finch

Dear Finch,

It's not made up, but you are free to think so.

Also, for the record, you do not "talk too much". Quite honestly, I find the way people constantly censor themselves abhorrent. I want to hear what you have to say. I mean that.

How far are you from the edge of the solar system now?

My childhood was what you might call . . . rural? We lived in a very hot climate—desert, in fact—and I've never quite gotten used to the *humidity* here. We did basically everything ourselves (which, unfortunately, led to my extremely independent nature and unwillingness to ask for help). My parents died when I was rather young, and I turned to a life of—well, I shouldn't say what *sort* of crime, because hello, Tolstoy. Let's just say I turned to a life of jaywalking and dog-earing book pages, yeah?

I knew I wanted to travel from a young age, so when the opportunity presented itself, I did. I traveled the world, Finch. I took whatever jobs were available. They were often revolting and grueling, but to wake up, sun or wind or rain on my face, and know I was utterly and truly free? There was nothing I wouldn't do to hold that feeling against my soul.

I made some friends. I lost far more. At some point, I decided to settle down for a while. That's where I am now: waiting until adventure grabs me by my arteries again and dares me to move.

Does something similar swim in you? I feel it might. As much as you might say you had no choice to be on a spaceship, you still agreed to go into the unknown. You are brave.

My day is . . . abnormal, I think. I'm pretty much nocturnal at this point in my life. I wake up around sundown, wander the city, find food, so on and so forth. Speaking of, download a recipe book, I'm begging you. *Microwaves for Dummies* or something similar. (I say this fondly.)

There's a small tea shop that stays open very late that I enjoy going to. I don't drink much tea myself, but I buy it for my upstairs neighbor. She's an old lady who enjoys the finer things in life. I wouldn't call us friends, as we rarely talk, but she seems to appreciate the tea I leave at her doorstep. I'm not really sure why I do it.

I too read and reread your letters before I respond. Also, I try to respond immediately after I awake (though I admit, it is usually night), so it is, in fact, Tolstoy who is keeping us from extremely late-night conversations, well into morning. Perhaps he knows we would be incessant and never shut up. Tolstoy, I entreat thee. Let Finch and I experience sleep depravity together. Call it a bonding exercise.

I print your letters and keep them folded in my breast pocket. When I am feeling lonely, I simply read them. I thank you for them.

Do me (and Tolstoy, I'm sure) a favor? Please sit down and have a frank discussion with your crew about how they're leaving you out. Report back to us when done, yes? The thought of you closing in on yourself up there makes me fit to tear myself to pieces.

Yours,
Aku

Aku:

Thanks my good buddy-man, but I'm not a ten-year-old on a playground, yeah? I can handle myself without getting into weird discussions with coworkers. I've been alone before. I can be alone now. Which, I'm not alone *anyway,* because I have you. And Tolstoy. Hello, Tolstoy.

I also have all these *books,* which I'm still perusing trying to find you. You're somewhere in these digital pages. I know it. Could you give me a hint, at least? I'd love you forever about it.

Actually, tell you what: you go tell that old lady you enjoy your silent friendship, and I'll talk to my coworkers.

Anyway.

I was reading today, and I learned about "Last Thursdayism" which I of course wanted to immediately tell you. The joke concept that everything was created last Thursday: all the planets, all of us, all our memories, everything. And that fake evidence was planted against it. It's funny. It's also kinda cool, like, nothing before last Thursday matters, yknow?

But then also we don't truly know what's out here, if all the evidence is false. Maybe we'll get swallowed by a giant whale. A space whale. Last Thursdayism. The whale was made last Thursday, too. If you talk to your friend, I'll talk to my crew and make Thursdayism my opener. Can't possibly go wrong.

What's your life philosophy, anyway? What do you hold to the highest belief? What spurs your decisions? Moral quandaries? Etc?

What would *you* do in the trolley problem?

I've been thinking about you, y'know. Mm, there was a better way to say that. Backspace backspace backspace. Um, I've been thinking about you trying to stargaze in a city big enough to have a midnight tea shop. You should really take a trip out to the country and stargaze there. Less light pollution. The difference would be astounding.

My family and I used to go on these like, backpacking trips, and we'd bring our shitty little cheap telescope with its terrible horrible no good very bad tripod (aside: no offense to you if that's what you're using, but if you get the chance to get a dobsonian, do it) and we'd set it up anywhere the canopy overheard cleared. None of us really knew any of the constellations or anything—in fact, I think Dad got the damn thing for like a dollar from a random yard sale on a whim—but it was nice, looking out to space and sharing snacks and stories. You should do that. Bring Alexandria. Or your old lady friend. I bet you'd love it.

We'll be passing Uranus soon. Goin' faaaaaast. Maybe you'll be able to see us. We're passing to the . . . um, left? Fuck, how do directions work in space? I gotta go ask someone.

STARBOARD. THE STARBOARD SIDE, MATEO SAYS. THAT HELPS A TON. WE'LL BE PASSING TO THE STARBOARD SIDE. POINT YOUR TELESCOPE *STARBOARD*. COME ON.

Jesus, that's not good enough. Let me find you some fucking coordinates so you can see me. Give me your coordinates so I can see you. Fuck.

Okay Ashraf was more merciful. He says that, since you're in New York, what you'll need to do is find Uranus with your telescope, then turn it about 3° West (or, as he initially put it, 3° back azimuth). We should be a little bitty dot if viewing conditions are good and your telescope is powerful enough. Even if you can't see us, you'll be looking directly at us.

Now it's your turn. Coordinates. Cough 'em up.

Ashraf is reading over my shoulder now so I'm gonna wrap it up, be seeing you (ha!) soon.

—Finch

My dearest Finch,

I'll start with the drumroll, eh? 37.6913° N, 91.0802° W. Come say hi. I'll be waving.

To be clear, I do not live at those coordinates. I'm going to them to be able to see you better. Little bit of a fly, but nothing major. Definitely worth it. And I borrowed a dobsonian telescope from a friend. We shall see how adept I am with it.

Also, do not worry about "better ways" to say things. It's okay. I've been thinking about you, too.

I did not manage to convince anyone to spend a mosquito—Filled night taking turns staring into space with me, but Alexandria promises she will next time she is in town. What snacks do you recommend? Milky Ways? Starbursts?

I did, actually, already know that the sky changes her appearance based on where you are. You should've seen the stars in the desert, Finch. There was no better way to feel *marveled*.

My telescope is set up. I know you won't get this letter tonight, so there is no sense waving to you, but here I am. Hello. I think I see you.

The grass is wet. I think it rained here recently. It's all cold and probably bad for my borrowed telescope, but I'm afraid I can't care at the moment. I definitely think I see you. Tomorrow night we will be looking directly at one another. Modern science is rather incredible.

Speaking of various sciences, you asked about my philosophy. I'm what you might call an old soul (and yes, I can hear your sarcastic gasp from here). I've thought of this very question for many sleepless mornings, and it ultimately boils down to this: Do no unnecessary harm.

I hate harming things. But I harm the plants I step on. I harm the food I eat. It is impossible to exist without harming something. And sometimes, harm takes the form of violence. It is unnecessary to kick someone while they are down. It is . . . perhaps a smidge more blurry when it becomes whether or not to punch a kidnapper in the face. The answer is yes, do it. Violence. It has its place. It is why I could never settle with Buddhism, unfortunately.

Do not mistake me, Finch: I am a gentle soul, not a harmless one. I have done more than I care to admit. I wish to never harm anything ever again. I know that is unlikely. The tiger harms the gazelle. The rabbit harms the grass. The tree root harms the clover around it. But they also help. There's this dichotomy, between harm and help. I think that's my philosophy. That suffering isn't always some great evil.

(Ah. And we are back to Buddhism.)

Do you think tigers would rather not harm their prey? Is it futile to apply morals to predators? What if I was a monster? Could you apply philosophy to me?

As for the trolley problem, it doesn't matter what I choose. I would never be content. I would always regret, either way. So another life philosophy of mine: avoid trolleys. Problem solved.

As an aside: those backpacking trips sound nice. Was your childhood filled with moments like that, or were those the metaphorical shining spaceships around Uranus?

Yours faithfully,
Aku

Aku:

WAS THAT A URANUS JOKE?! AS AN ASTRONAUT, I AM APPALLED AND OFFENDED . . . Good job, man!

Okay I'm pointing the telescope to you RIGHT NOW.
Heh.
We're looking at each other.
:)
Oh uh, Mateo says hi.
Also Ashraf.
And Meredith.
And Chloe.
And Todd.
And Tolstoy. Hi, Tolstoy.
Well, Aku, you've got an entire spaceship full of people looking at you. But especially me. Especially me is looking at especially you.

I'll come back and finish this letter in a little bit. Right now, I kinda just wanna look.

Okayyy, oky okayy okqy+!! Soooo thr cool thing bout chemiss is they can make ALCOH9L!!! WOO!!!

Meredith made ue alcoohol qnnnnd I maybe drank a LOT. Itwas VERY GOOD. We SAT AROUND nad TALKED like FREIENDS. Are u proud of me Aku?? I havefriends right now.

Ur my friend tho, ye? Ur my best friend. Best friendd ve ever had. Ur thr best man. Can't wait to finishh thsstupid mission n get home n then we can hangoutproperly. Ill take u to a park so u can use m awesome telescoope an we can see the eholesky together. Ill point out evry cool star shape thingy for u. Show u the whooe hewvens. Yknow I deeam bout u soetimes. I dream but u a lot. Whtdy look like, Aku? I wannaknow.

Todds wants me totellu what im doing rightnow so: I am sitting on thr floor n staring through the telescopr. I'm lookim at u :) can't look away, fck. Ur captiviajg.

Ohhhh meresith mqde more shots sooooo I gotta go, I cant make more sentnences so ill send another later, gnight sweet dreams love finch

My dearest Finch,

I am so so glad you had a good night with your newfound friends! See? They truly weren't so bad. I hope you drank plenty of water, though. And also encouraged *them* to drink plenty of water. Is one of you the "mom friend"?

Wait, that's silly, I know the answer. Tolstoy is the mom friend. Hello, Tolstoy. And the poor thing can't make you drink water from Earth. How he suffers.

I enjoyed staring at you as you stared at me. I think I felt it in my soul.

As for how I look, I'll try to be straight—Forward. I'm 5'11". I have extremely long, black, voluminous hair that I should really cut. Trimmed dark facial hair. Um, I dress in jewel tones. I've been told I have soft eyes. They're brown. I'm brown. What else? My hands are slender. I'm running out of ways to describe myself. I like going barefoot. I like bangles. I pierced my ears the moment I learned it was something I could do. I'd love a tattoo but haven't decided on one yet. I think, mostly, I just look somewhere between hulking and soft. What do you look like, Finch? An eye for an eye.

Please drink some water.

Yours,
Aku

PS, I dream of you, too.

Aku:

I am going to die. My head is throbbing and my mouth tastes like . . . like if cheese were made out of cardboard but still via the same scientific processes. Blegh. Also everything is too bright and too spinny and fun fact if you throw up in space it pushes you back a little. I hate it here.

Anyway, back to where we were. Philosophy. I'll do my best to answer coherently with my head against the toilet seat. Maybe I won't throw up on the handheld, eh?

As someone who got in a few fights, I think . . . I don't know, ugh. Hold on.

Okay, um, violence definitely has its place, right? Like, I'm not peaceful. Don't think I've ever been peaceful. But the thought of peace always sounded kind of nice. To not have to worry about anything, not be constantly on-edge about things that don't even matter, like . . . I see the appeal. I'd happily give up anger for peace, y'know?

Hold on again.

Okay, okay, doing better. Feeling better. Okay. So. Back to this. As for whether or not we can apply morals to tigers, nah, I don't think so. Survival is a different category that I don't have a philosophy degree to get into. Monsters are different, though, right? Because to be a monster is to contain the implication that you understand right from wrong, so, I'd say morals apply to anything that can understand them. As for my personal philosophy, I think that the only things that matter are what we make matter. Like, I

Hrm.

Okay, so, it doesn't count as backspacing if I never finish the sentence. So I'm just . . . leaving that there. Call it an art piece.

Uuuuggghhhh. Why did none of us think to bring nausea medicine up here. Maybe Meredith can make some.

Also, for the record, the friends situation fixed itself. I didn't say a *word,* so things worked out like I knew they would. Point one Finch, point zero Aku. I'm winning.

As for how I look, I'll go give this to Chloe and let her tell you because A) I'm bad at describing myself and B) I'm going to throw up again.

Short. —C

Hi this is Meredith!! Finch came up, handed Chloe the handheld, said, "Tell him how I look," then proceeded to throw up in the sink! He's still over by the sink! Throwing up! What a guy! Anyway I saw what Chloe typed and I knew that wouldn't be good enough for the much-discussed Aku so I took the handheld from her so I could tell you! :D Finch really isn't that short, maybe just a little. He's still taller than me and I'm 5'6" so maybe that gives you an idea? Hold on I'll ask Todd bc he likes to measure things!!

Finch is exactly 1.75 meters tall. EXACTLY. All of his measurements so far are perfect, non-infinite, non-weird numbers. However, he does not like being measured, so I must be sneaky about it. I will let you know if any more interesting measurements come about. This is Todd.

Meredith again!!! Finch has dark hair that he keeps on the long side of short! It's a little wavy! He's always got a five o'clock shadow and has kinda bushy eyebrows and his face is so squishy! I can't say anything to his personal style because we all wear regulation clothes but I think he purposefully ordered his a size big and likes them kinda baggy! But in like a cool style way! He swears he only brought two pairs of hearing aids but I've seen at *least* eight different colors so I think he might be painting them! He looks fit but he's actually not (no offense Finch!!!) and usually goes around in socks :) Also he literally ALWAYS has this handheld with him wherever he goes! He just looks at it all the time and waits for a response from you and it's so so cute! He also

Feajflak ajfj faiofaeioewa fa kjrkej kfdjd VOICE CONTROL ACTIVE. NOW LISTENING. PLEASE SPEAK UP . . . PLEASE SPEAK UP . . . back give it back guys come on all i wanted was for chloe to tell him how i look and i did no you didn't you told him finch was short well finch is short i'm not short yeah you kinda are can i please just have the hand held back now nah you gotta catch it i can't catch it it's because you're short i'm not short and i will tackle you fine fine take it back sorry we were just playing i know i know hey shit you guys turned the speech to text on oh shit really yeah really look ha hi ah coo oh my god look how it spells ah coo ah coo ah coo it's funny because you're named after a bird and coo is a bird noise ah coo hello from us all ah coo alright i'm turning this off now boo let us embarrass you more hey ah coo last night

Sorry, they were playing monkey in the middle. I was the monkey. My handheld was the middle.

Um, I don't remember where we were and now they're all begging me to talk to their penpals too so I think I gotta go? Now that the awkward initial phase is gone, I have to figure out how to make time for everyone. Ugh. Might have to start waking up early. Shudder.

Anyway, can't wait to hear back from you, man.

—Finch

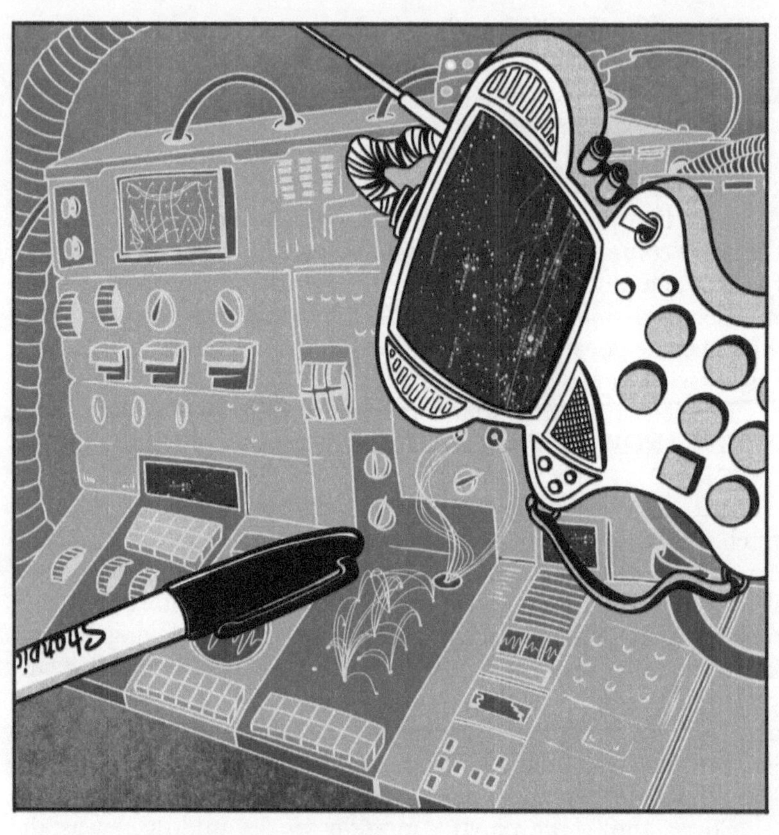

hort i'm not short yeah you kinda are
please just have the hand held back n
can't catch it it's because you're sho
and i will tackle you fine fine take it b
ust playing i know i know hey shit yo

Dear Finch,

It makes my heart so warm to read all of that. I'm glad you have friends to mercilessly tease you and try to embarrass you. Perhaps the space journey will not seem so tiresome now.

It will please you to know I've convinced Gladys, my neighbor, to stargaze with me tonight. We are sitting together on lawn chairs in our backyard. It's funny; we've shared this house for years, but only now are actually talking. She says hello.

She's lived a fascinating life, Finch. She was a war nurse and saved countless soldiers; she even married one. She's fought in every civil rights campaign she's been alive for, and she's still feisty. She has a margarita right now and sunglasses on. At night. This woman is truly living her best life.

I've told her all about you, and she thinks you're fascinating, too. Which you are.

Her husband was a hobbyist UFO researcher, and she is incensed that I have not asked you about them. What are your thoughts on aliens, O astronaut? I know you said you were on board to translate potential alien languages, but I truly cannot tell if that was a joke or not. Or if I'm allowed to tell her that, if you aren't joking, after all.

I personally think there are definitely aliens. Gladys and I have been talking about this topic for the past hour or two. She's more skeptical than I am, but that makes for interesting conversation. I can't imagine that we are all that exists in this giant universe. How lonely that would be. How sad. For humans to have no other life to share their discoveries with; their music, their poetry. I can't speak to the logic of it; I just can't bear the sadness of being all alone. As much as I wish you here beside me, there is at least comfort in looking to the night sky and knowing someone is looking back. I hope I spark that comfort in you, too.

I must admit, I've been researching the mission you are on. Just a heads up to Tolstoy, someone forgot to pull one of the original announcements with the missing crew member's name in it. I definitely did not look up her name to see if she was arrested, or whether espionage was ever an official charge. I, like a good law-abiding citizen, left well-enough alone. I can't promise others will do the same.

So you'll be back in a few years' time, yeah? That gives me plenty of time to plan our park trip. I was thinking we could go backpacking. I bet you'll miss things like trees. We can bring a shitty telescope and throw it into a stream, if you're truly sick of space by then. Or we can set it on fire and dance on its ashes. I'm pretty good at waltzing. Do you know how to waltz, Finch? If you don't, time to start learning, as I *will* be initiating one when the moment feels right.

Gladys says the waltz is a boring dance for boring people, and I respectfully disagree.

Is there somewhere specific you want to go? Besides Rome. I can take you anywhere. We can fly.

Gladys needs another drink so I'll be going to make that. When will you be passing Neptune? And Pluto? It's insane to think you're almost outside our solar system. Check in with Tolstoy to keep that existential dread at bay.

Yours,
Aku

Aku:

I adore Gladys. Tell her to adopt me as her grandson right this instant.

I don't know how to waltz. I'll start practicing.

You know where I'd really like to go? Alaska. Just, the middle of nowhere. Nothing around for miles. Inaccessible by vehicle. A danger to myself and others just by my own lack of survival instincts. I want to be entirely surrounded by nothing with you.

You asked about my childhood a few letters back, and I was purposefully ignoring it then, and I still am now, but I'll mention my dad always held Alaska in front of him like this giant goal of his. To go to Alaska. His metaphorical green light. Guess it rubbed off on me.

Anyway, yeah, passing Neptune soon. God of the sea and all that. Do you have an Akkadian word for sea? Also, Mateo told me that it takes light two and a half hours to reach Uranus, so were you looking at me that long? I was looking at you that long. Like, I know that means we were looking at each other in the past but like, I need to know we both at least actually saw one another. It feels important.

Yeah, hold on, I'm gonna go talk to Tolstoy for a bit. BRB.

OKAY I AM BACK. So guess what? I woke up early this morning! I got my socializing out of the way so I had time to sit around and read your letter and write back! Ayy! Look at me, planning shit and getting shit done. Someone should be proud of me.

Aku, I've been taking so many pictures as we pass by things. I can't send them because ~data restrictions~ but I'll show you when we get back. Things look so different up close than they do through a telescope, or even through the eyes of a rover. It's insane and honestly makes you feel really tiny. But in a cool way.

Okay so re: aliens . . . I totally, 100% believe they exist. I've not been given any like, special information, and neither has anyone else (or so they say), but I can't believe we're truly alone, either. Even if the alien life is single-celled organisms, it still counts. There have to be space bacteria, and that's enough for me. (But supersophisticated, space-traveling aliens would be DOPE.) Like, you should see what I'm seeing. This vastness. We can't be the only things in it. It's just statistically unlikely.

OH HEY! I got one of Meredith's stupid chemistry jokes today! All this studying is paying off! And yet, I still cannot figure out what books you have written, and you refuse to give me any hints. The hunt continues. I also found a cookbook and successfully made rice this morning. Everyone was very impressed, so I now have (another) new station on this ship: cook. Please recommend some cookbooks, I'm flailing over here. "Cooking for a crew of six on board a spaceship with very specific rations for dummies" or something.

I could go ahead and start supper, actually. Everyone is writing their penpals. I got to say hi to them all yesterday and they seem nice! Very diverse crew. One of them is a professional gamer, she's Mateo's penpal. I think her name was like, Avalon? Or something? I'm bad at names. She was talking about making a space-themed video game and was asking for separate experiences to make it more authentic. It was pretty neat. We'll have helped with a video game! Meredith's penpal is a retired man who really enjoys fly fishing and gardening, and the two of them get on well. I know one penpal was a veterinarian, another was essentially a cowboy, and I'm forgetting the others but you get the idea. Wanna know something weird? They all like, put work before their penpals. Can you *imagine?* Pffft. Really though, they write maybe every other day? It's super casual for them.

. . . looking back, I think maybe I interpret friendship different than they do. Maybe that was my issue going in. Note to self: everyone's brains function way different than mine.

Yeah so basically, I'm intense and they're not. Not to say they don't like their penpals! They totally do! Just in a different way.

Oh god, am I too intense for you? Are you more like them? I'm sorry if I'm coming off too strong, I can scale back. Do I need to scale back?

No, no. You would've said something. I know and trust that you would've. And since you didn't, I can safely assume I am okay. Phew. Having a *day* here.

Anyway. I think we're speeding up one more time before we get past our solar system, then we'll kick it into hyperdrive. Can't wait for that, because that just puts us that much closer to being done and being back home and being with you. In a park. In Alaska. Start making plans.

I'm gonna go see if I can figure out mac-n-cheese. Tell my new grandma Gladys I said hello.

—Finch

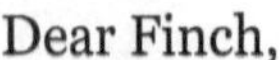

Dear Finch,

I'm sure Gladys would happily adopt you. I have tea to drop off on her doorstep tomorrow, so I can ask then. I would've dropped it off tonight, only I was excited to write back to you, so I might have decided to hold off a bit.

I like to end my night with you now, generally. I do all my errands early in the night, then I get out the telescope and write to you and look up until the sun begins to rise. Then I'll go inside and dream. And since I am already out here tonight, the tea must wait until tomorrow.

Yes, of course I stared at you for more than three hours. I stared all night. I'd stare all of tonight, too, if it wasn't raining. As it is, I'm just sitting outside, listening to the noise, and thinking of you. Do you miss the rain?

I would absolutely tell you if you were too intense, or if you bothered me at all. But you don't. You're wonderful, and everything you say to me, I treasure. Perhaps the rain is making me a smidge dramatic. You'll just have to deal with that. Also, I'm looking into an Alaskan backpacking trip as we speak.

The Akkadian word for sea would be something like abzu, only that is specifically freshwater. I'll let you use it, though, and will only complain a *little*.

Okay so . . . cooking. Cooking is easy. *Baking* is difficult. For cooking, just experiment with things you have, see what works and what doesn't. Cooking is truly an entire science project on its own. I believe in you. When in doubt, find a recipe. One day, you won't need them.

I once cooked all the time, back when my parents were still alive. My mother and I would stay in the kitchen all morning, kneading bread and cutting fruit. It was a ritual of sorts, a way to bring on the sunrise. There is little more intimate than making food with those you love. It has been a while since I cooked anything.

We used to make *everything* from scratch (since I know you are going to ask me to elaborate). We grew many plants for the sole purpose of feeding ourselves, and our neighbors raised a breed of cattle. We would trade between us to supply entire meals. Making bread, however, involved all of us. The grain had to be harvested, the seed separated from the chaff, the chaff separated from the bag. Then it had to be ground down, and *then* we had flour. Repeat the process, ad infinitum. It might sound repetitive, but there was something about those repetitive tasks. They calmed our hearts, or at least, they did mine. I would listen, and mill, and the world seemed narrower, somehow. You and I should make bread, Finch. I'd be interested to know if it soothes your soul, too.

We could make bread in Alaska.

The lightning looks beautiful right now; I wish you could see it with me. Maybe you can. Do you see it? As you look through your telescope that is so much more powerful than mine? Do you see the backs of the clouds where I see the fronts? If so, did you see that lightning? It was beautiful.

Yours,
Aku

Aku:

There you go again with the poetics, man. I swear I'm thisclose to figuring out what you wrote.

Also you are correct; I was *absolutely* going to ask you to tell me about cooking with your family. It does sound nice. It sounds very nice. Sorry to hear about your folks, though. Same boat.

I saw the lightning. You're right. It was beautiful.

This morning has been weird. Mateo and Ashraf are like . . . holed away. Haven't seen them all day.

Hey quick aside, in a non-bad and non-judgemental way . . . you wanna bet they're finally getting it on? Because I'm picking up vibes, man. I think they're gonna kiss and then proceed to be super lovey and gross for the rest of the mission. I need another barf bag. (Because they're lovey, not because they're gay. If they're gay. I'm cool with gay. And more than gay! Not that the other letters are somehow *more than* gay, it's all equal gay, but like gay as a general descriptor and not gay as in homosexual. I swear I'm not homophobic. I'm digging myself into a hole here, aren't I?)

Look. I just think Mateo and Ashraf would be cute together. That's all. I hope they're banging. They deserve it.

Iiiiiii am going to switch topics now, I think.

Rain sounds nice. Yeah. Sorta miss the rain. I should talk Tolstoy into downloading rain sounds for us. Pleeeeeease, Tolstoy?

He sent a raincloud emoji!

Okay so when I get my nonexistent raincloud, I'll turn on the noise and we can listen to the rain together. Maybe I'll smash pasta up and make bread from it, and you can do that too, and it'll be like we're making bread together. Weird, gross pasta bread. It'll be amazing.

Did I tell you I successfully made pasta? I mean, it's all prepackaged bullshit but I made it! In a pan! And only had to follow 98% of the directions! I'm learning!!!

Everyone liked it, or at least *said* they liked it, which is quite frankly good enough for me. Not like I can get worse, right? (Don't answer that.) I'll keep trying to make pasta until I can't get it wrong and everyone is so sick of pasta that they beg me to make something else, and then I'll make pasta one more time just to be an asshole. Mwahaha. Then I'll make like, grilled cheese or something.

I took a *really cool* photo of Neptune. There are all these variations of blue on it, and a spot that looks like the eye of a birch tree, and there was a cool lens flare into deep space. It's so amazing, how nature fractals and repeats itself out like that. Abzu. Aku. The planet Neptune. Fractaling and repeating beauty, huh?

Backspace? Backspace backspace backspace???

Anyway. I think we're all about to try and break down the door to Mateo and Ashraf's rooms and get some blackmail. Wish us luck!

—Finch

My dearest Finch,

Ha! I hope you have fun on your escapade! I also hope they end up together. It would be very cute, no? I too am, how you say, "cool with gay."

Your bread sounds, respectfully, awful. No pasta bread. I'd have to block you. Pasta, however, sounds lovely, so you've earned your respect back. You terrify me in such a lovely way, Finch.

It is still raining here. The lightning is still beautiful. What's your favorite weather? Mine is fall, when the wind begins to blow cold and a storm threatens the horizon. It feels like I can do anything. I felt that exactly earlier today, when I first stepped outside into the night. It was perfect. I went into town and met a man about a Dobsonian telescope. I know you're beyond my sight now, even with this, but it feels closer to you, somehow. Perhaps I will take a few months and build one from scratch, make it the size of my house. I could take pictures of you and you could take pictures of me. We'll swap after.

Gladys says she will happily adopt you if you bring her tequila, by the way, since I won't. (Not that I'm against it, I just don't have a valid ID. Long story.) We drank tea together this morning and I told her about your latest letter. She is invested in you, it seems, though perhaps in a different way than I am.

I've been looking into Alaska, and it seems lovely. There are almost infinite places we can go to escape everyone else. We might have to fight off a bear or two, but you're well-trained in that sort of thing, yes? (I'm joking.) It will take a ridiculous amount of planning, but lucky for you I have a ridiculous amount of free time. Do you like mountains? We could climb a mountain. Or two. Or ten. Why stop at Alaska? Once you are assuaged, we could move on to Canada. Or settle down in Alaska, build a cabin, invite Gladys. Make a life for ourselves away from space stations and people that don't quite get us. We could have a pet of some sort. Oh, did you ever have pets? I once had many cats.

Judging by my calculations, you should be hitting hyperdrive tonight, yes? May the sun guide you home.

Yours,
Aku

Aku:

We have hit hyperdrive baybee!!!

Mateo and Ashraf are acting weird, but it's probably because we found them making out HEYOOOOOO!

It was a really weird like, teary makeout session that we all immediately felt awkward about barging in on. But we still got blackmail. I regret nothing.

Also can I like, tell you something and you promise not to take it the wrong way? I dreamed about you. We had a house together—Alaska I guess—and we were making breakfast in the kitchen. You were showing me how to knead bread. Then it started lightning and thundering outside, so you tossed off our aprons and pulled us out into the rain and we waltzed. The rain was cold, I remember that much. I don't remember the last time I stood in the rain. Go run in it and describe it to me?

I don't like to linger on things, but Tolstoy says it's good to sit with my feelings, so here goes: I really miss the rain. Like, I didn't realize that until I was dreaming of it, but now it's all I can think about: you and me, dancing in the rain. It's bouncing around my head. Grass under our feet. Soaked through. Laughing. These bouts of loneliness keep hitting me square in the chest, y'know, when I think about all the things that make Earthen life mean something. When I think about what awaits us out in space.

I really used to think nothing mattered, and maybe it still doesn't, but we can assign things meaning. I think Earth means something. I think you and me in the rain means something. I dunno. Maybe Mateo and Ashraf need to go run through the rain or something, maybe it would make them less teary.

I don't know how they're doing. If they're doing?? I've never been in love, like, I wouldn't know where to start with it. Have you? Shit, I never asked if you had a girlfriend or anything. Do you? I feel like you would've mentioned if you did. I don't. For the record. Girlfriends just . . . never worked out for me.

My head feels weird. Probably because I fell asleep at the telescope, pfft. Bad decisions on my end. Or maybe it's the hyperdrive. Anyway, I'm gonna hunt down Meredith and demand she make me a Tylenol.

—Finch

My dearest Finch,

I like that dream. I'm imagining it, us, in Alaska. I bet the rain is even colder there.

Well, it stopped raining here, but I took a short flight to a nearby storm. It was pouring in the way that soaks you to the bone, where you have to look down to get a clean breath. Rain falls over your face, across your nose and lips, like the sky itself wants to kiss you, all cold and wet and trembling. Rain that makes you feel like you're truly part of the world, holding on just like the trees and grass. It would be hard to dance in this weather, but I think if we held each other close enough, we might manage to not leave enough room between us for rain on our lips.

I've been in love. A few times. It's different, each time. The way two lives intertwine and mesh is a beauty all on its own. I don't like the phrase "fell out of love", but I'd say my time with the others was simply over. Our lives had phased together and back apart, and there is nothing wrong with that. Some loves are meant to last for eternity, and others for a short while. I've not yet found an eternal *romantic* love, but my (platonic) love for Alexandria transcends time.

Love feels like . . . wanting to experience everything together. Wanting to share all these little things about yourself, and learn theirs in return. It's sleeping in and being content with doing nothing but laying in bed together. It's just wanting to live, together, and being kind to one another. That is love. And if you sprinkle in some romantic intention, then you have romance. Or at least, that's been my experience. Others might be different. What's the closest you've been to love? Or was every relationship something withering?

I've got plenty of water, if you need to quench some memories. I'll be counting the days until I can show you myself.

Yours, eternally,
Aku

[Untracked unofficial transmission, side channel 0.0027m]

Hey Aku!

This is Tolstoy. Don't have long. Finch can't see this. Please don't respond. This will delete after five minutes. I know you're as hopeless as he is and you have your handheld with you at all times. I've attached the official mission briefing. The one Mateo and Ashraf now have and Finch does not. No you're not allowed to tell him. Yes I hate it too. Never mention this to anyone.

I'm sorry.

Tolstoy

[Attachment]

[End transmission]

Aku:

Mateo and Ashraf are doing like, marginally better. They're attached at the hip and suuuuper sleep-deprived, from what I can tell, which is terrible because I am not responsible enough to be the captain. Help.

Chloe is teaching me how to not let plants die, so I've got that going for me, at least. Maybe soon I'll be able to not let the crew die, either! Yay! (That's sarcasm.)

Chloe and I have gotten closer. She's very . . . deadpan, but I understand her humor now. She even corrected my attempts at French eighteen times, so I think we must be good friends.

Todd let me touch his Legos! Oh god that sounds like a euphemism. I swear it isn't. He taught me illegal builds. Which are a thing. That exists.

Anyway, I tried to convince Tolstoy to let us modify a few things to make a zero gravity shower in here and he said no, so I won't be standing in fake rain and thinking of you anytime soon, unfortunately. Something about electrical and drowning hazards. He's a stick in the mud, but we love him anyway <3

So here's a thought: picnic in a storm. Let everything get ruined and have a great time anyway. Roll around in puddles or whatever. It'd be great.

Re: my past relationships, they just . . . I dunno. I was never really like, into them? I wanted to be. So badly. But none of my girlfriends ever made me feel . . . alive, I guess? They were all short—Lived. I never felt like I could really *talk,* y'know? I'm adding so many filler questions. I'm sorry. I don't have a good answer. I just don't do well dating.

Like um, I remember I was dating some girl, Jennifer I think, and we were at a movie. She kept like, making our hands touch by reaching for the popcorn at the same time as me so I just . . . stopped eating the popcorn. Which is a *huge* deal for me, because movie theater popcorn is one of the best foods in the world. But I didn't want to hold her hand. I didn't want to even touch her, really, and when she tried to kiss me during the romantic part, I uhhhhh miiiiiight have thrown up on myself instead. I blame the copious amounts of soda I was drinking sans popcorn. She was sweet and all. She walked me home and even offered to go buy me medicine. I just. Wasn't into her. It's always been like that.

People get weird when I tell them that. They're like "ohhhh you poor thing, you'll find the right person eventually" and it's like . . . why does it matter if I do? What if I don't, huh? Am I suddenly a failure? Why should my life revolve around love? If I find someone I can't live without, they'll be my best friend for eternity. I'll kiss them under the starlight and make them breakfast and dance with them and whatever. And if I never find someone, I'll still stare at the stars and I'll still make my friends breakfast and I'll still dance with whoever I want. My life isn't lesser for never having experienced this very specific sort of *love.* It's dumb that people act like it is.

Not that you act like that. Just went on a little tangent, sorry.
Hey.
Can I tell you one of my like, greatest fears?
I'm absolutely terrified that I'll find love one day, and be so wholly unexperienced that I won't realize what it is until it's too late.

My other greatest fear is giant squids. Fucking terrifying little bastards.

Anyway, thank you. For describing the rain. I swear I can feel it on my lips.

—Finch

My dearest, my lovely Finch,

It is so, so very good to hear from you. It always is, of course, I just wanted to reiterate that here and now. I love hearing from you. It makes my entire year, every time.

Tell Tolstoy I said hello, and thank him for allowing us to communicate and whatnot. He's pretty awesome. Is he reading this? You're awesome, Tolstoy. I'll always be here for you and Finch. Always. Not going anywhere.

I'm so glad you are growing closer with your team, and also, shush. You would make an excellent captain. I'm sure Mateo and Ashraf will find their solace soon. In the meantime, you can maintain peace with your friends by simply being your incredible self. Maybe you could make Lego plants, allow Chloe and Todd a meeting point. Just a thought.

I'm sorry that your dates have been atrocious. I can relate: I once stepped on my date's foot a total of thirty-seven times by the end of the night. It's a wonder they didn't lose a toe.

Dating shouldn't be as hard as people like to make it. It's just having fun with a friend that you also want to kiss occasionally. Nothing so scary, after all. If it would help you, when you get back, I can show you how a date is meant to be. So you know.

Is your morning routine still the same? What has changed on your ship? Spin me a story, Finch. I want to hear it all.

I heard the transmission sound in the middle of the afternoon, aka when I was asleep, and I woke up and could not fall back to slumber. I read your letter over and over again. I'm out looking at the stars now. It was so hard to wait until now to respond. I'm pretending I can see you. I think that twinkle was your smile.

I'm working on that giant telescope, now. I found an abandoned property deep in the woods. I cleared the overhead canopy a bit and am working on making what, essentially, will be an observatory. The Finch Observatory. Because I will be observing you. There are actually finches nearby. I think of you every time they sing. (Well, I think of you all the time, regardless, but especially when they sing.)

I wish I could attach drawings. Have I mentioned I like to draw? I used to be very bad, but I practiced for years and can now almost draw a stick figure. (That's a joke.) I draw the finches when they stay still enough. I've filled notebooks with them. Or, I will, anyway. I don't know if you like birds, but I do. I don't see them often, what with my sleeping schedule, so when I do it is a real treasure. Their songs are beautiful, and more learnéd men than I know what they're saying. I wonder if that makes them less beautiful. The knowing. Knowing what it truly means, how the sound is created. Does it ruin the magic? If it does, I hope I never learn.

I acknowledge your greatest fear. I understand it. My own greatest fear is that I will wake up one day and realize that every decision I have made was the wrong one, and now it is too late to fix them. But can I tell you something, Finch? I don't fear that with you. I know every moment I spend writing to you and reading your words is something I'll never regret.

What amazing sights can you see? Any nebulae? Galaxies? Regale me. Please. Give me enough to read for the next year. Write me for months. Write me every three minutes and fifty-six seconds. I think I crave you.

Yours, undoubtedly,
Aku

Aku:

You've done a lot in the uhhh single day since I heard from you. Like, holy shit, man. Did the spirit of productivity suddenly possess you? Can I have some? Or else whatever dosage of Adderall you're taking, damn.

Right now, if I look outside, I can't see anything. When I finally got Mateo to stop being cagey and weird, I asked him, and he said we're going too fast. That's it. Wouldn't meet my eyes or anything, so maybe I should start thinking about regretting barging in on him. Doesn't matter anyway, though. Our route is pretty coordinated to take us around any obstacles that would be, y'know, *interesting* to look at. However, since we hit hyperdrive, I've had vertigo. Ugh. I was hoping it would go away, but it's looking like our local chemist will have to mix something up so I can stop trying to navigate in zero gravity with my eyes closed. It's rough. Gonna stop looking outside again now, it makes the nausea worse.

Um, daily routine is pretty much the same. Mateo and Ashraf both said goodbye to their penpals, which, boo, but to be fair they never wrote them anyway. Plus they have each other now. I can't even *imagine* the sorts of talks Mission Control is having to give them about appropriate behavior. I wonder if some poor intern is stuck on camera duty watching weird gay astronaut sex. Hahaha I bet it's Tolstoy. Ashraf is quieter than usual, but, eh. This place could do with more quiet anyway.

I've been entertaining myself by sneaking into Todd's room and replacing single bits of his Lego models with illegal builds instead. It's fun hearing him find one. I miiiiiight be driving him to madness. Whoops.

Beyond that, I've been trying to bake a bread you'd be proud of. Don't let all of this sound like true productivity; it's mostly me avoiding my real responsibilities and being bored. Eventually someone is going to call me out about it, but right now I'm using the vertigo as an excuse. Though if Mateo and Ashraf weren't lost in each other's eyes all the time, I'd have already had a talking-to.

Aside, we really gotta think of a ship name for them. Matraf. Ashteo. The Captains. I need something shorter since I'll likely be making jokes at their expense a lot. (Again, because they're in a relationship within eyesight of me, not because they're both guys.) Look, my next bet is gonna be Meredith and Chloe. Technically I think Meredith is already married so that's probably not gonna happen, but I am 100% still taking bets. What's your bet? Mine is that they won't get together, but that tensions will skyrocket between them and by the end of the mission they won't be able to stay in the same room without blushing. I'll bet you three loaves of bread and a Lego wheel I stole. Your turn.

Why am I only taking bets for same-sex couples, you might ask? It's because literally every person on this entire ship gives off ~vibes~ except Todd, who is an enigma. He has Lego—Fucker vibes (I say, respectfully, because he scares me). In other news, I found a book all about cuneiform, which feels like something you'd know about. Can you write in cuneiform? Could you teach me?

Re: your greatest fear, I get it. And while you may regret your decisions, I cannot find fault in them, because they led you to this reality, where I get to pester you about breadmaking and thunderstorms. End justifies the means and all that.

I think I'm gonna go have Meredith make me that motion sickness medicine now, I feel kind of awful. If I feel better I'll send another message later on. Hopefully one with enough words to last you a year, as you put it.

—Finch

I think I have a fever. I had that dream again. I say again like I've told you about it. It's 3 in the morning if time had any meaning, and I'm sitting here, sweating like I'm on the goddamn sun, feverishly writing. Maybe I have a fever. I might. I feel like I might. I had the dream again. The one where you kiss me. You crave me. You crave me. I crave you too. What do you look like, Aku? What do your lips taste like? I think I have a fever. I had that dream again. I dream about kissing you. Do you dream about me, too? Is it really you in my dreams? Can dreams travel across space? Oh, Mateo is knocking on my door. Says Tolstoy sent him. Why are you still here, Aku? Why are you still putting up with me? Is it so I still have someone to dream about? Sometimes I dream about more than kissing you. Oh, I disabled my backspace key. I forgot. Mateo is really banging on that thing, so I gotta go. I think I love you.

Yours,

Atticus, Atticus, Atticus, take my real name, take the name no one else can have, it's yours, my Aku, your Atticus Atticus Atticus, I bet I wouldn't even mind the way it sounds if it's your lips forming it, call me Atticus when you kiss me in my dreams tonight

Hi! I Am Going To Murder Tolstoy For Sending That.

Oh god oh god oh god. Please forget that, I claim insanity, I was all hallucinatory and sick and please don't stop talking to me I think I'd die

Oh god that's not helping, I'm not helping the situation, I'm sorry

My dearest Finch,

The vertigo sounds awful. I don't suppose you have some ginger around to fix it, do you? I've found that's always effective. You could even bake it into some of your horrific pasta bread.

Ashteo sounds significantly better than Matraf. At least, in my opinion. But, of course, The Captains is the best ship name of all. Also, I'll definitely take that bet. I'll bet you that Chloe and Meredith wind up drunkenly kissing one night and never mention it again. I'll bet you an extra practice date on it, even. However, I am harboring a secret, second bet: that you'll ultimately get bored and play matchmaker. If I win that one, you have to write me a smushy, fluffy romance novel. Not novella. *Novel.* It has to rot my teeth with sweetness.

Literally everyone on the ship gives off "~vibes~" do they? Literally everyone? Every single person? Barring Todd the Lego Fucker, of course.

I do know cuneiform, though it has been incredibly long since I've needed it. I cannot guarantee its accuracy. When you return, we shall gather clay from the soil and I'll teach you how to write poetry in it. What is your favorite poem, Finch? This is mine:
I felt like kissing the swords
because their glimmer
reminded me of your smile.

I adore poetry. Ah, perhaps I have said too much, since you are still looking for something that I have written. (Hint, hint.) There is something about the way poets use language that never fails to cinch the edges of my heart. I hope you do not loathe poetry. Or, perhaps, I do, because then I could spend our correspondences convincing you that poetry is beautiful and splendid. I could put a new poem in every letter. Things about stars and your eyes. Maybe I could write you some new ones, if you so desired.

I've been working very hard on the observatory. It's really coming along. I can't decide if you'd like it because of its nature, or if you'd hate it because of yours. You hate the stars. I get the feeling you really adore stargazing, though. I love stargazing, because it is as close to seeing you as I can be. Hello, up there. I'm waving.

Do you like coffee? I can practice making it your favorite way, that way I'll have it perfected when the mission is over.

How is chemistry going? And your plants? And the mission?

Yours,
Aku

My Atticus,

I think we must share dreams.

Yours, as always,
Aku

Atticus, Atticus, Atticus,

I do not want to forget it. Your feelings echo themselves through my soul. I am here. I want to talk to you forever. I am yours, as I have said, over and over, since the beginning.

Yours,
Aku

Aku:

Ah okay okay, message received, loud and clear. We are not talking about it. We are continuing on as if it never happened because that is what I asked for.

Wait no, fuck, I don't know. Fuck.

See okay here's my issue, here's why I've been staring at the screen for like two hours now. This . . . doesn't feel like you? You don't hide things like that. Like, if you wanted to ignore it, you'd tell me that. This just feels like you didn't read the thing at all, which, maybe Tolstoy never really sent it and now I'm just incriminating myself. If that's the case, ignore this, too, because I am *not* telling you what I said.

But like, the other option is I was all "hey I might have gay feelings about you" and your response was to uuuuUUUUUGGGGHHHH I DISABLED MY BACKSPACE KEY, *FUCK*.

Okay fine, *fine,* now you definitely know and you can help me through whatever-the—Fuck this is because I've *never* fucking felt this way and I don't know what to do, man, and you're my lifeline and you're . . . ignoring it? Or else you read it and you're still over here spouting poetry to me about kissing me. You're either cruel or oblivious or trying to say you have gay feelings about me, too. But Aku, my dude, I'm too new at this. I don't *get* the undertones, I don't *get* this pseudo—Flirting shit. I've never even dated a guy. I need you to just *tell me.* Please. Tell me to fuck off for eternity. Tell me you're secretly married and your wife says we have to stop talking. Tell me anything. Everything. Tell me what's going through your head, please, I'll be normal about it, y'know, I'll tone it back or down or whatever I need to do. Just let me know.

—Finch

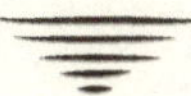

Aku, fuck, man, c'mon, literally less than an hour after I sent that whole whiny spiel you're over here telling me we share fucking dreams, Aku what am I meant to do with this, what do you expect me to do

hey did you know if you cry in space it just sorta balls up on your eyes and then you have to go find a rag or a towel and when you do that you have to face other people and avoid questions because you do, that happens

Why the three parts, huh, you should've gotten all of those when you woke up as per usual. Why the torture, genuine question. Why send them like it's been a week and not just one single

. . . you're goddamn *joking*. No. No no no. Aku, tell me it's only been a day for you. Tell me it's been one single day since I had that fever. I swear to fucking god.

My dearest Finch, my Atticus,

I waited for all three messages that I knew were coming. Unfortunately, I have been told I cannot answer your question. Which, probably, answers your question.

I finished the observatory. I wish you could see it.

Yours,
Aku

PS: to be fully and entirely clear, as you have asked: I love you. I love you. I love you. Dream of me. I'll dream of you, too.

Fuck.

end part one

Okay hey hi, it's me, Finch, again. Why the fuck did I Judy Blume that. "Are you there, Aku? It's me, Atticus."

I just called an emergency meeting, which I definitely am not authorized to do, but everyone showed up anyway and it went something like this:

Me: Hey, we're fucked.

Chloe: Actually, I think that's only Ashraf

[Here she high—Fived Meredith]

Ashraf: Oh God

Todd: It's alright, buddy, they're just—

Ashraf: You know.

Me: What do you mean *I* know?! The fuck do *you* know?!

Ashraf: Mission Control met with me and Mat the other day.

Todd: *Mat?*

Mateo: Did they meet with you, too?

Me: No, I just—So I was messaging Aku—

Everyone else: ha gay

Me: Shut the fuck up.

Chloe: When you gonna finally tell him you wanna bone?

Me: I—

Meredith: Oh, don't be so crass. Our little bird is just in love is all!

Me: Well—

Todd: Yeah, when are you going to confess your undying love?

Me: I did that when I got sick from Meredith's motion sickness medicine, thankyouverymuch.

Meredith: Sorry again—wait, you *what?!*

Me: Moving on! The response was weird from him, and then he sent two more messages instead of looping them all together, and it felt off so I was thinking 'damn it's almost like he's not receiving these all at the same time' and then it hit me. He isn't. Right?

Mateo: Right.

Me: He can't tell me how long it's been.

Chloe: How . . . long?

Mateo: We're moving ridiculously fast. Time is traveling differently for us.

Meredith: Like, how different?

Ashraf: They won't tell us, either.

Me: He asked me to write him every three minutes and fifty-six seconds, which feels sort of hyper-specific.

Chloe: Barf.

Todd: Are we assuming he wants daily communication? Or is he meaning hourly? That changes my math.

Me: Um, probably nightly.

Todd: So the implication is that for every three minutes and fifty-six seconds here, a day passes there.

Meredith: But that's like . . . what, just under twenty days every hour?

Todd: That's 365 days for every one of ours.

Me: I'm sorry what.

Todd: A year is passing there for every day we're on this mission. Supposedly.

Me: We hit hyperdrive three days ago.

Chloe: So that's . . . three years back home. Fuck.

Me: Wait so, Mateo and Ashraf, you were both sobbing or whatever when we found you after your meeting. But you didn't know the math. Which sort of leaves the question . . . what did they *tell you?*

Mateo: You're not going to like it. And we're not supposed to tell you.

Meredith: We could always mutiny.

Mateo: You wouldn't. And besides, I'm not going to keep it a secret. Not now. Um, they told us that we'd be gone long enough that no one we knew would still be alive when we returned, basically.

Todd: Jesus Christ.

Me: It's a four year mission.

Chloe: *Fuck.*

Todd: That's over—

Meredith: Don't. Don't.

Me: He built me an observatory. He named it after me.

Meredith: Oh God, Paul—

And now everyone is crying in their various rooms. Fun times.

So great. Great. You love me, huh? And I probably love you. And here we are. When I get home to see you, you're gonna be a headstone. If I'm lucky. That's almost fifteen hundred years, Aku. You'll be a blip, and I'll be some fucking relic of the past. Todd and Mateo are trying to figure out how to reroute controls but . . . I dunno. I think I know how Laika felt.

You wanted every three minutes and fifty-six seconds. Here I am.

You should probably let me go, you know. It's just gonna hurt us both. Long distance wasn't meant to be like this.

I'll never see the rain again. Fuck.

The one time, the *one time* I actually feel something about someone, this happens. Fuck.

My favorite poem is a piece of a song. By the way.

I am a man with a heart that offends with its lonely and greedy demands.

What's your favorite song, Aku?

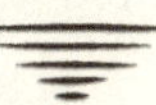

Sorry sorry I'm meant to be letting you let me go. I'll shut up now and go water my stupid fucking plants.

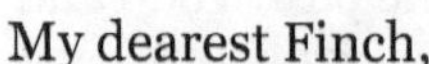

My dearest Finch,

I am not going anywhere. I will be here when the sun explodes and consumes the Earth. I'll watch it with you. I refuse to let you go. If I was going to, I would have done so the moment I learned of your true predicament. Yet, I am here, by choice. I love you, Finch. I love you on purpose.

My favorite song is a lullaby my mother used to sing me. I'll sing it to you when you return.

All my love,
Aku

Aku:

Hey, no, *no*. You're supposed to be out here telling me goodbye, not lying to make me feel better. Over a thousand years, huh? You'll still be there in a *millenia?* You gonna cryogenically freeze yourself? This doesn't make it easier. It doesn't. God I wish that could be true. So bad. I walk off this stupid spaceship into your arms and all the buildings are different and the cars are different but there's my same old Aku, same long hair, same soft eyes, same strong arms. I know them from a dream.

What happens when you die? One day, one day in like, four months *max* you'll just stop responding. Don't waste your life on me, Aku. You spent three years building a monument to a man you will never meet. Let that be all you spend on me.

—Finch

My Finch:

Forgive the tone of this letter, but I truly do not remember you being in control of my decisions. What bit of letter, perchance, gave you the impression that you are in any way in charge of what I do? What gives you the right to command me to live my life as something other than what I desire? Am I to live by *your* desires? Would that not be, inherently, building not a monument but an entire *testament* to you? One of flesh and blood and heart and brain? Is that what would please you? Unfortunately for you, and very fortunately for me, I do not *bow*. I will do as I please, and now and forevermore what pleases me is to love you. So I will continue to love you, and write you, and dream of you, and you can, respectfully, *fucking deal with it*.

The Finch Observatory looks *spectacular* and sometimes I let classes take field trips to it. Nights remain for me.

Yours, forever, eternally, undeterred,
Aku

Aku:

Yeah. Okay. Understood. As long as you know what you're getting into. I'm a mess. Especially right now but also always. I'm impulsive, I act on emotions, I don't understand personal space, I constantly lose things, I dog-ear pages, I eat oreos middle—First, I think punctuation is fascinating, I don't know how to talk to people, I'm sarcastic, I'm mean, I'm so many things, Aku, so many things you'd be better off without.

But thank you. For staying.

Um, we can't wrest control back. There's a code we can't crack, and no one will help us. So. Right now, we're stuck. Tolstoy is the only one actually responding to us, and he still can't give us answers because they won't tell him because he's too likely to tell us. He said no one who ever worked with us directly knows the code. I guess that would induce too much guilt. *Wonder why.*

I want to know who approved this mission. I want to strangle them with my bare hands. Then push them out an air lock in deep space. Watch them implode.

I've gone from sad to angry, mostly. I'm still sad if I think about it too hard—if I think about *you* too hard—but more than that I'm pissed. Meredith is married, for fuck's sake. Glad Mateo and Ashraf have someone *on the spaceship,* because otherwise they'd be fucked, too.

Todd is just. Building and unbuilding things. I think I need to go help everyone but I'm not sure how. It would feel fake, to try and cheer them up. Maybe I just need to do what you do and just . . . listen. Just be there. Maybe that's my purpose here.

I'm gonna make pasta, bring it to each one, and let them cry with me. Yeah. That's what I'm gonna do.

Aku, what's happened in the three (now four) years since we exited the solar system? What's going on in the world? Enlighten me.

—Finch

My Finch,

I fully understand what I am "getting in to", loving you. Both eyes open, ramu.

Well, as for what has been going on, um . . . I sort of . . . tend to stay away from every piece of news there is. I'll go ask Gladys, she's more likely to know.

She says, and I quote, "Fuckin' idiots with fuckin' power doin' fuckin' shit-all about it."

So. The usual?

Oh, I know a very small asteroid hit somewhere in rural Texas and tests are now being run on it, but the city refuses to relinquish it, so all these scientists have to go there instead. And there are no hotels, so the locals are setting up pricey rooms for rent. I'm not picking a side here, but the whole situation is sort of funny. I hope a scientist and a cowboy go on crazy adventures. Enemies to friends. Maybe lovers? Who knows.

"A president got murked." There you go. That seems more like what you were looking for. No I don't know the details. If it doesn't affect me directly, I've found it best to not bother knowing.

I could talk your ear off about safety regulations in observatories, though. Or the most basic of physics on space travel. I've become, as of late, obsessed.

Did you know that the universe is very big? Learned that one in a picture book.

I've been thinking of you a lot. Dreaming of you. My dream-you never quite has his feet on the ground. You're always floating, just slightly, like you can't seem to shake that space off of you. But it's okay. I'll make sure you don't float off.

There have been two stray cats around lately, one black and one white. I've been feeding them, and I think I might keep them. Any name suggestions?

In my personal life, I've been keeping things pretty much the same. I'm still nocturnal, I still keep up the observatory, though I do have a staff now. Sometimes I'll audit astronomy classes at the local college, as long as they're at night. Some of the professors know my name now, which is . . . strange. I don't entirely *like* being known. I'm more someone who prefers to exist at the edges of other people's vision. You would be the exception. But, anyway, I've been invited to some sort of conference a few states over. Just to listen and be there. I don't see any reason why not to go, so I suppose I will. I still don't care for large groups of people, but if it means I get to learn more about space, then I will "suck it up".

I've also been very into pomegranates as of late. The small grocery store I frequent started selling them again. I suppose they're in season?

So, to disclaim . . . I have this issue where my body can't actually process nutrition, so I have a supplemental diet. As in, if I ate nothing but pomegranates and bread and salads and steaks and everything else, I'd be malnourished. But . . . I still like baking. I still like the flavor of food. I *adore* the surface tension of pomegranate seeds. I can't be the only one, right? Biting into a cluster of pomegranate seeds is probably the most satisfying thing in the world. Except perhaps biting into you. Rawr. (That was to make you laugh. Did it work? Did I use rawr correctly? It only recently was accepted into the dictionary.)(I'm joking again. Was your linguistic heart appalled?)

I do wish I knew what your voice sounded like. Did you have some awful high school band with a single, scratched CD that I could hunt down? Or perhaps a home video of you faceplanting into the ground after jumping from a trampoline? I'd accept anything. As long as it's you.

Tell me if I come off too strong. I know how terrifying feelings can be, and I also know I've had years to process mine whereas you have only had days. You are still coming to terms with this paradigm shift. It's okay. I'm here to listen. I'm your friend, first and foremost and always. We can laugh the awkwardness off. I like laughing with you.

Stay safe. Stay whole.

Yours,
Aku

Aku:

I'll do you one better. Tolstoy said I could, just this once. When you get this, tune a shortwave radio to 2343kHz and place it by your handheld. It should work? Tolstoy says it will work.

—Finch

AUDIO TRANSCRIPTION OF RADIO MESSAGE, FREQUENCY 2343KHZ

Finch: "Hello? Uh, is this thing on? Oh God that was lame."

Chloe: "It was."

Finch: "Hold on, Aku, I'm moving to somewhere less people-y." [Shuffling noises. A door closes.] "Okay, I'm alone now. With the telescope. Heh, um . . . hi! Hi there! I'm—I mean, I'm Finch. You know that already. I um . . . shit. I should've made up a script. I just—you asked about my voice and I thought, 'oh, duh, aliens send radio signals or whatever all the time so why can't *I* do that?' so here I am. Um. Doing that.

"I'm usually way better at talking than this.

"I'm just making a recording and Tolstoy is going to air it when he gets the whole thing. This is apparently super against the rules or whatever so we can only do it this once. Um, how do I sound? Do I sound . . . good? I've never thought this much about my own voice, ugh.

"Um, this can't be super long so I uh, I just wanted to say um . . . ahem. Okay. So. I . . . You . . . God I'm so sorry I don't know how to start. I thought about it so much and now that it's here I'm—yuck. Okay. Trying again.

"You already know that I . . . I think I might . . . y'know . . . love you. And this is like, the one time you get to hear my voice. And I know it's not true yet but the thing is . . . it will be. I know that. I'm just going to collapse into your gravity. I fucking orbit you, Aku, I—

"I just. For the record. Because one day, it will be true and you deserve to hear it:

"I love you.

"Sorry I sound so shaky. I love you. I'm terrified of that. I'm somber about that. I love you. Fuck. Every day it's closer to true. It's inevitable. You're inevitable.

"Um, I gotta—I gotta wrap this up. I'm looking through the telescope. I think I might see you. Heh. That's a—That's a dark joke.

"Um, so . . . goodbye. Finch, signing off.

"How do I turn this thing—"

My Finch,

I've been sitting here, staring at this lake near my observatory. Just breathing, and thinking.

I have traveled deserts. I have stared at the stars in wonder on freezing sands, and I have gazed into the tempest at sea and known my own death was inevitable. I remember the first photos of galaxies beyond our comprehension, I have witnessed birth and death and everything in between. Usually these things bounce against my skull, this constant reminder that everything is filled with a level of awe I am incapable of fully experiencing. I can't hold my breath forever, after all. Some days I pick up my wrench, or my paintbrush, and it feels so microscopic that I might not bother doing it at all. What would it change, in the grand scheme? What would this drop of paint on a page do besides capture yet another likeness of you? I've refused to look at photos. It wouldn't seem fair. My point is, you stare at me from a hundred similar faces on the pages of a book and it's infinitesimally small. Yet I sit here, and the waves lap at the shore, and somehow nothing is greater or more important than the way your voice sounded. I don't feel small. I feel . . . more whole, maybe?

None of this made sense. I'm trying to say thank you. I pray the stars do not take you from me before I'm allowed to kiss the shakiness from your breath.

Yours, yours, yours,
Aku

Aku:

Well, hell. Got me feeling things over here. I'm shit at saying the sweet and soft and nice things so just . . . yeah. Towellin' it up over here.

We're actually rounding on our first official stop, some

exoplanet they're letting us name. However, we're all frustrated and angry, so *Fuck the International Aeronautics and Space Administration* is what it's looking like so far. We considered naming off every country's space program, but that would be too long a name. So IASA it is. I tried to amend "But Not You Tolstoy" and we decided Tolstoy could be one of the moons.

All our current estimates are showing it as a very fucking cold, lonely place that none of us wanna be. No water to speak of, but liquid nitrogen is everywhere. Chloe says it's hard to tell yet, but that there may be plant life that's not carbon-based. She tried to explain it to me, but I'm like, sixteen textbooks behind where she is.

Todd is making sure our spacesuits are up to the extremes and Meredith is preparing sample collection. Mateo is preparing landing gear and Ashraf is "making sure no one does anything dumb". Which . . . fair. I was indeed planning on doing something dumb. However, I feel I should at least be granted the freedom to *try*. I might still try. (I'm definitely still going to try.)

Tolstoy ratted me out >:(

See, that's not fair, in my opinion. Since he monitors messages as we type them, he gets to read and respond way faster than you get to. Sure, he has to look at a screen and watch like, single letters appear every hour or whatever, but I still think you should get the same luxury. But noooooo, it's a "hazard to the mission" because I'm "unstable" and could "jeopardize international secrets". Well, fuck them, it wouldn't be an issue if they didn't make me some weird sci—Fi time traveler. I should get a little rebellion. As a treat.

Ashraf had a talk with me about how we can't take out our anger on the various space programs, mostly because it only harms us, not them. I wish I could harm them. Does that fall under your "necessary harm", Aku? Am I justified in wanting to rip their skulls from their spines? I think I could, right now. I think I could do it. I think I could rip their arteries out with my teeth.

I have been put in time out.

Mateo gave me a pillow and said, "Well, it's not regulation, but you can always punch the shit out of this." So at least I get to do something constructive with my pissed-off-ness.

Punching the pillow pushes me back, too. Like it's parrying every hit. I hate space.

I've gotta get out there on this mission. If I have to stay in here a day longer I'm going to explode. I need to see new scenery, walk on something with gravity.

Can you meditate? I can't. It's always like "Silence your thoughts" and I can't get any farther. It's constant up here, man. Got ADHD on one side, anxiety on the other, and who-the—Fuck-knows-what happening in the center. Like the worst frat party you've ever been to, all hours of the day. Loooouuuudddd.

You know, I used to love looking out windows on road trips. Kinda helped quiet all the noise. But these windows are different, and I stare into space and it's just louder. Actually louder. I have to turn my hearing aids off because I start getting . . . I don't know, feedback? Like weird fucking whispering. Creeps me the hell out. But then everything is muffled and I can hear my own thoughts too much again. Got any tips to make me shut up in here? I want to be present and mindful and whatever. It's just always felt unattainable.

I'm gonna punch the pillow some more then convince Ashraf I'm okay enough to go outside. Or beg. I might just beg.

I think it's the control, really. That someone else is making my choices for me and I don't have a say. I have no control. None of us do.

Tolstoy should just go ahead and diagnose me with depression too, I think. Oh, great, he said that's outside his jurisdiction. Why is everything in my head buy one, get six free?

Breathe, Finch. Breathe.

I probably should sit this one out. I'm gonna go tell Ashraf that and then just focus on existing. Maybe. Or maybe I'll just think about you. Maybe I'll reread everything you've ever sent again. Maybe I'll take a nap and dream of you. You're really pleasant to think about.

—Finch

AKU IT WORKED I GOT ON THE PLANET I TOLD ASHRAF I SHOULD SIT THIS ONE OUT AND HE TOOK IT AS A GOOD SIGN AND SAID IF I CHANGED MY MIND I COULD COME SO

I DID AND I BROUGHT MY PISS BAG AND PISSED "FUCK YOU"
ON THE FROZEN GROUND, I HOPE THEY FUCKING SEE IT
WITH THEIR STUPID GIANT SPACE TELESCOPE AND I HOPE
THEY DIE KNOWING THEY WILL NEVER EARN MY
FORGIVENESS AND THEY BETTER BE BURIED IN
UNMARKED GRAVES BECAUSE THE MOMENT IM BACK ON
EARTH IM FUCKING COMING FOR THEM

Also I'm under Ship Arrest for a while.
Worth it.
I love you.

—Finch

My lovely little rebel:

I know I'm likely meant to be scolding you, but I think you did
amazingly. I would have loved to have been there. I can imagine
the fire in your eyes. I'm painting you now.

Be a nuisance to the space programs. Be a thorn up their ass
for the next millennium. Make them pay.

Alexandria says she is proud of you. She moved here recently.
She does that sometimes: moves to be closer to me for a few years.
She's painting a mural on the outside of the observatory. She says
it's going to be you.

I've started a community garden by your observatory. The kids
seem to really like it, and I enjoy growing things. Did you ever
garden? It is so nice to just walk outside and grab ingredients. I
feel in control, like you were talking about. These things in my
hands, everything I could need. (Besides you, that is.) I go outside
and it's like the flowers bloom, all at once. They bloomed this
morning. I think they were telling me I'd hear from you again.

What are your favorite flowers? I'll plant rows and rows of
them. I'll make paint from their petals. I'll dry them and bathe in
them. Was that weird? It felt weird. I'm trying to straddle the line
between romantic and strange, and I'm not so sure I'm succeeding.
Oh, well. Full speed ahead, I suppose. I'll drown in their perfume,
and the barest mention of you would breathe me back to life.

There, there. I'm done now.

I love you, too. If that wasn't obvious. If I haven't said it enough. My sweetened criminal, I love you. Would you like me to say it every time? I can. I love you. I love you. I love you.

The only help I have on meditation is that it doesn't have to be silent, sitting down. Find something you can focus on, and make it into meditation. I paint. Perhaps you could write ancient languages? You adore them so. Alexandria binds books. I knew a man who would box. Find your moment that you can live in, then live in it. Sometimes the moment is cross—Legged with *ohm* on your tongue. Sometimes it's digging holes in the dirt. It's all the same, really.

I'm sorry about the whispering. I don't know how to help with that other than to simply say I am here for you to vent to. It sounds horrible.

Have you encountered any alien languages yet? Or are you allowed to tell me? Do not respond to this question at all if it's the latter.

I might have found a place in Alaska for us. I'll have to go visit it myself, but it's some sort of hunting lodge on a great many acres of land. The sort of place we could get lost in and never return. I bet we could even find a cave and let the Earth eat us raw.

I'll be honest, caves sort of terrify me. I don't know what it is exactly, but being in a cave feels like being actively digested by the universe itself. So while I *will* go into one, for and with you, I'd vastly prefer not to.

Lately things have been hectic, from what I can tell. I still avoid the news, and so does Alexandria, but every time we go into town, more and more shops are closed down and boarded up. I hate watching cities die. I hope things turn around, but we stocked up on tea. Just in case. Gladys is still doing okay, by the way. She says hello.

I hope you are feeling better, and that your imprisonment does not last too long. I wish I knew your coordinates. I'd love to see your handwriting.

Yours,
Aku

PS: Yes, I would consider teaching the space programs a lesson to be "necessary harm"

Aku:

I am still under containment. They're calling it containment instead of space prison, but we all know the truth. They keep stopping by and telling me how they're on my side and this is just for the logs, and how my door definitely isn't unlocked and how there totally isn't space hooch in the fridge with my name on it.

Anyway.

You found us a place, huh? Barely been together for a few weeks and we're talking moving in? I accept.

Aside, damn, how are we keeping up with dating days? It's been *years* for you. Also . . . we *are* together, right? I just sort of assumed. If you want freedom since, y'know, I'm gonna be up here when you die of old age and all, I get it. I don't mind. You just gotta promise to keep sending me letters. You're what's keeping me sane right now.

I've been buzzing about the future a lot today. Meredith's penpal died. The old guy. The fisherman. It was coming, we all knew, but this is . . . the first of many. We only know because his daughter sent another message about it. Please promise me that when you die, you'll have someone tell me? I mean, I'll know. You won't send a message one day and I'll know. But still, I'd need the confirmation.

I don't like this thought road. I'm taking another.

I agree with you on the caves thing. Caves *are* creepy. I'm an above-ground sort of guy (and yes, I see the irony). I just feel like something bad is going to happen every time I'm in one. Like, maybe there will be an earthquake and the entrance will close up, or maybe I'll take a wrong turn and get stuck, or maybe I'll run into some long—Forgotten creature of the night so old it doesn't even have a name. Y'know. Rational, normal fears.

I'm sorry to hear about your town. I've seen plenty of run-down old towns, with the signs of shops still hanging up like it was too sudden to properly close, and it's just . . . sad. I hope your tea shop stays open. If I were there, I'd be going by and buying their entire inventory every day, just so you could show up on restock day and get the tea you love. (Tell Gladys I said hi back.) Actually, I'd buy every tea *except* your tea, and then you could go by and get that tea, and together we'd keep them in business. Teamwork.

I miss dogs. Random, but I do. Miss their stupid little excited tails and their slimy tongues and their pure unbridled love. Can we get a dog? Raise it on the Alaskan land? With your two cats (who, if it is not too late, I would like to name Timmy and Steve) and maybe like a ferret or something I dunno. A cool ball python. A pretty bird. A little family, you and me and our petting zoo.

We're on our way to our next planet now. Or well, the ship is on its way and we have no say in it. Maybe I'll behave well enough to lull them once more into a false sense of security. Maybe. It *would* be cool to find evidence of some form of alien language (which, no, I have not found yet). Maybe then I'd have some sort of bargaining chip against the space programs. Yeah, I *gotta* get on that planet.

I gotta admit, that short time I was out of the ship, it was nice to see the stars again. When we're going as fast as we are, you can't see them. You can't see anything. I guess that's why we can't get control of the ship; we couldn't even maneuver it home. I wonder if they can see us with their fancy space telescope. I bet they can't. I missed the stars.

They're different, this far out. I swear, Aku, I was standing there with my bag of piss and . . . you know that feeling you get when you're walking down an alley alone at night? Like someone is just . . . staring at you? I get in my head too much, Aku. I start thinking I'm seeing things.

I've decided to start cataloging what's going on, not *exactly* a memoir but not too far off. I think I might let the others write in it, too. We could each give our own views of events, then when we finally get back to Earth, we won't have to do a debriefing. We can just throw a flash drive at the lead asshole's head and go *home*.

Um, coordinates of the piss curse are RA 5h 48m 59s | Dec -2° 26′ 30″. Horsehead Nebula but sorta . . . slightly off. If you want to see my handwriting for real. If you have a telescope that can.

Okay so, on to your questions that you asked:

Do I garden? Not really. I used to forage with my dad, but I wouldn't say we ever tamed any food to eat. We just found it where it already was. Sometimes we'd spread the seeds, but it feels a bit too chaotic to still be called gardening. Like, rows of tomatoes and peppers and squash and whatnot wasn't in the cards for us. We moved around too much. But we'd go into the forest or along the ditches and he'd point out all these plants or mushrooms to me, and we'd grab as many as we could and stuff them in the bowls of our shirts before heading back to wherever we were staying. The world was my garden, I guess. You're getting a bit more backstory this time around, hope you appreciate it.

What's my favorite flower? Honeysuckle. That one was always my favorite. It was always easy to identify, and I could find a bush and snack all afternoon. Not that it's much of a *snack,* just that it was something sweet to do. There was one place we stayed with this rusty chain link fence around the boundaries, and I would climb over it to get to the honeysuckle on the other side. Wound up needing a tetanus shot when I slipped and got gouged by a stray wire, and I didn't get to climb over anymore, but while it was there, it was nice. I would still go by every day and watch the bush grow closer to the fence, until I could ball up my little fist and shove it through and grab handfuls. Like the flowers missed me, too. Anyway, yeah. Honeysuckle is my favorite.

Should you say *I love you* every time? Yes. Say it every time. I love you.

I'm gonna go try to convince everyone that I should be on the next planet and I can be trusted not to piss off or on anything else.

Don't die on me this year.

—Finch

PS: I can't wait to see this observatory.

My dearest Finch,

You were a nomad. Are you still?

And yes, we are together. You are my . . . boyfriend? Partner? Comrade? Frère d'armes? You are my very significant other, whatever that entails. Call us what you will, I am with you until the end of time. I adore you.

For me, we've been together over a decade. That probably strikes you as strange. Take a while to process it. And before you ask, yes. The nights sometimes seem to drag on forever without you.

You have been with me, all these years, you know. You are in my midnight coffee. You are in every brick of my building. You are this noble bird that Alexandria painted on the side of the observatory. You are these blooming honeysuckles. Every action I have taken, your spirit rested in my hands. I have not been alone, not since I have known your name. These are the vines that wrap around me. Look: I am an ancient statue in a forgotten garden, lost to everyone. Lost to everyone but you. It is all the sweeter, then, that we love each other. Time goes by. We can watch it together.

How is your not-memoir going? I'd love to read a bit of it. And space has always been terrifying. I would ask the others if they feel it, too. Don't suffer this alone.

As for current news, it appears there's some sort of war going on. (When isn't there a war going on?) I'm afraid I don't know the specifics, as I quite frankly do not care outside of a historical perspective, but that has mostly been what I've overheard. That, and a specific bird species has spontaneously started laying orange eggs where before they were blue, and no one quite knows why. I personally am more invested in the birds.

Do not misunderstand; I care for people. It is the political conflict that does not interest me. For such an advanced species, humans truly are horrifyingly stupid, sometimes. How many lives is a philosophy worth? Apparently, thousands.

Also, I promise you that *if* I die, I'll have someone tell you. I am sorry to hear about Meredith's penpal. May his soul find the rest it deserves.

Do you have a grief counselor? *Are* you the grief counselor? I'm beginning to doubt the efficacy of the choices for this mission (no offense). There should be someone trained in these sorts of things there with you. Or is it Tolstoy? How old is Tolstoy? I'm curious. Hi, Tolstoy.

I'm still sorry you can't see the stars. I've studied it, you know. By all accounts, you should still see them, merely slowed down infinitely. But you can't, and I don't know why. A decade of study, and I don't know the answer. I'll find it, though. I've got an entire library of astronomy textbooks, not to mention all the engineering and various other ones. I've become a walking encyclopedia, all because I keep thinking about you.

I liked the backstory. Here's some of mine:

I was a poet (if you hadn't picked up on that). One night, when I was but a young adult, my town was attacked by a band of outlaws. They pillaged and slaughtered a lot of us, my family included. They were all set to slaughter me, as well, when one recognized me. He was, apparently, a fan. They forced me to make a blood pact and become one of them. I betrayed them at the earliest possible opportunity, of course, but that does not change the fact that their blood is in my veins.

There. A backstory. Or, part of it. The worst part. You can have the worst parts of me, if you'd like. Any part of me. They're all yours. I bet you could run your hands over all of them, and I'd come back with your name where my god's should be.

I really can't beat that line, so I'll talk to you soon. I love you.

Yours, completely,
Aku

Aku:

Fuuuuuuuuuuuuuuuuuuuuuuck.

Yeah, I should've guessed you were a poet. That makes sense. Also: damn, that backstory. I'm sorry. Really. I am. I'm here if you want to talk about it more. I'm also here if you never wanna mention it again.

Over a decade? Time isn't adding up here. You're hinting to me again, aren't you. Jesus.

Also: over a *decade?* A DECADE. We've been together, for you, for over a *decade.* Yeah, I don't know how to feel about that, you're right. I'm picking apart these emotions, and I feel overwhelmingly . . . sad. You sure you wanna date me? You sure you sure?

And that makes you . . . what? Over forty? I'm gonna stop

thinking about that one. Tolstoy is a bit older than me, I think. So as old as you. And yeah, he's technically the acting grief counselor, and I am the liaison.

I've decided, in the single day (for me) since we've talked that I'm going to try to find at least one positive every day. So today I am happy that Chloe smiles at me so genuinely, even when she teases me. It's nice.

I'm out of space prison, and of course you can read my mission log. I'll be honest, this one is mostly not-me, since I was put on house arrest and all. Gimme a sec, I'll copy paste the good parts.

Okay some of it was voice so I had to break it up so it was easier to read. Keep in mind it's aimed at the bad guys. Commencing.

[MISSION LOG 1]

This is Finch Davani, starting more specific mission logs in the hopes of bypassing debriefing. We just left Fuck IASA, our newly-minted exoplanet. We all still hate you.

Fuck IASA, with its eleven moons, is an icy giant. The surface is well below freezing, and it appears to be nitrogen-based. One of the moons is named Tolstoy. The others are One, Two, Three, Four, Five, Eight, Thirteen, Twenty, Moon, and Pluto. The human body temperature is enough to melt the ground a small amount. There was no detected life, or signs thereof. Space is creepy.

Samples were collected quickly and quietly, after a brief foray wherein I was made to sit and wait for them to finish. Mateo guarded me and was definitely not holding back laughter.

[Here I cut some parts]

After this, I was taken into the ship and locked in my cabin as per protocol. I sat and thought about my actions and told all that I regretted them. I, however, did not truly. You deserved it and far worse. I was freed after what I assume was a due process hearing by a jury of my peers.

[Cut]

Switching to voice. Chloe, do you have anything to say for our first mission log like I told you?

Chloe: Yeah. Tell them to suck a dick.

Me: Duly noted. Thank you for your contribution. Todd?

Todd: I would happily put Lego in all of their shoes.

Me: Good thought. Meredith?

Meredith: They can choke on my foot up their ass.

Me: Inspired. Mateo?

Mateo: What they said.

Me: C'mon.

Mateo: Uff, fine. I'm going to make them all into dresses for their moms to wear while I fuck them.

Me: Jesus fucking *Christ,* man. *You* need therapy, not me. I'm proud. Um, Ashraf? Bring us home?

Ashraf: I hope they cryogenically freeze themselves. I'm going to come by with a sledgehammer.

Me: Beautifully done. First mission log successful. Say bye everyone. Ah, they're all flipping the recorder the middle finger. Enjoy that. Signing off.

[END]

So, yeah. There's that. And to answer your question: I guess yeah. I am still a nomad. I keep thinking about Alaska with you. I should start learning some plants I could forage, or at the very least *attempt* to forage and cause our grisly demises instead.

Ugh. Feedback loop again. I'm going to bed. I love you dearly.

—Finch

My loveliest Finch,

I would never hint about time things to you, as I have been explicitly instructed not to and would never break the rules. Obviously.

And yes, I am sure I want to be with you. Until the end of time, my love. You'll just have to deal with me and my strange notes and ramblings and displays of affection until then. You're going to come home, and I'll have three bookshelves full of drawings of what I think your face looks like, and you'll just have to come to terms. (So if you'd like to give me a more detailed and accurate description of your face, I'm all ears. Well, all ears and one pencil eagerly waiting to sketch.)

Unfortunately, my tea shop has closed down. It was inevitable, I think. These things always seem to be. Regardless, I will miss it. The workers kept me company on many a dreary night. I picked up a few extra things that I most certainly don't need, but I can never quite resist the siren call of good tea and tea accessories. I got a matcha set, complete with handmade chasen. I have unpacked it and am staring it down. It's beautiful. I can't wait to make you tea.

I once despised tea, you know. I didn't understand it. It was always, for lack of a better term, *half-tasting,* as if the flavor never fully saturated the water. Then I had tea with Alexandria, and I learned that it is more about the act of sharing food with someone than it is about the tea itself. I believe we've discussed this before. You and I, sharing food. It would already mean something if you lived here. It now means, instead, the entire world, since you are leagues away. I think I'd sell my soul to share breakfast with you.

Well, with my yearly insipid attempts at wooing you aside, I suppose I must update you as to the goings-on of the world at large. (I hope you appreciate this; I rather despise the news.)

There *is* a war. It's official now, or, as official as these things can be. It seems very all-out, with many countries I've never heard of (though do not take that to mean something it does not: I frequently misremember countries. I could have sworn Yugoslavia was still enduring.) and a lot of violent posturing and speeches. There's some form of attempt at forced enlistment, but it is backfiring horribly. I do not know what the war is about. For as many articles as I've read, and as many programs as I've watched, I've yet to receive a single, solid answer. In my experience, that generally means it's over trivial matters. For everyone's sake, I hope it is over soon.

Gladys and I have been drinking cocktails and listening to the radio announcements over it. She's just as chagrined as I am. If you were here, we'd all run away together.

She says hello.

I am tired, Finch, of the world. It is selfish of me to say, but I want you here so badly it makes my bones ache. I want to scoff at politicians with you, draft dodge with you.

For now, complaining via letter will have to do.

I love you.

Yours,
Aku

Aku:

Great. Great. So the time dilation is getting worse, then. Things are worse. I hate this. I hate this. I hate this.

Shit. Fuck. Shit. I'm cool. It's fine. I'm cool.

Um, your tea shop. Sorry to hear about that. I know how much you loved it. I guess the war ran it out of business. Sucks. It all sucks.

Also: *insipid?* You're calling your flirting *insipid?* It's the most inspired thing I've seen since Monty Python.

This is hard. This is harder than usual. Ugh. Breathe, Finch. Everything will be okay.

Um, my one positive thing today is that Mateo has this little curl of hair that never lies right. It's always making an escape for his eyes. It's very Clark Kent of him.

I can't be negative, because you don't get to hear from me very often because batteries aren't endless, but I also can't sit and pretend to be all positive since you're my best friend and I'm not gonna sit here and pretend with you. So we can do attention exercises together, yeah? Let's talk about something that isn't the war, or the stars, or the goddamn *noise* in my ears, or the future, or the lack thereof.

My face.

Uh, I'm kinda chubby in the cheeks, I think. I've got like, tan skin and this dark beard I try to keep trimmed, and a mustache and all that. I'm thinking of shaving the beard and keeping the mustache, if only to upset everyone else on board. Er, big curvy nose, bushy eyebrows, dark brown eyes. I've been told a lot that my eyelashes are "unfair", so they're like, thick and luscious, I guess. My hair is long and dumb. Goes to my chin, never does what it's supposed to do. I dunno, man, I'm not some Adonis, some epitome of masculinity or beauty. I'm just kinda me. I look like a person. I mean—of fucking course I look like a person, right, because I am, but like . . . like, I'm a very human—Looking human. I've got a lot of flaws that sort of play together nicely, I think. I've been told. I've got really nice lips, if you ever wanna daydream about kissing them. We can set up a scheduled time to daydream about it together.

Is that sexting? Did I just reinvent sexting??

. . . do . . . do you uh . . . *wanna* reinvent sexting?

I WANT TO BACKSPACE THAT SO BAD BUT I CAN'T BECAUSE I DON'T DO THAT BUT GODDAMMIT I REGRET SAYING THOSE WORDS. NOT THAT I'D REGRET SEXTING YOU JUST THAT MY MOUTH WAS BEFORE MY BRAIN. THE CONCEPT OF SEXTING IS TERRIFYING. I DON'T KNOW WHAT I'M DOING. PLEASE FORGET I SAID ANYTHING.

NOT THAT YOU'RE TERRIFYING THOUGH BECAUSE YOU'RE NOT IT'S JUST THAT I AM IN GENERAL TERRIFIED OF SEX LIKE I DON'T GET IT LIKE I'D BE WILLING TO TRY BUT IT SEEMS OVERHYPED AND WHAT IF I DO IT WRONG AND THEN YOU HATE ME LIKE WHAT THEN

Ahem. Having a real normal one over here. Backspace backspace backspace.

Aaaaaaanyway. We haven't given up yet here. For the record. Just so you know. I'm getting home to you, no matter what it takes.

Um, I have space hooch in the fridge. I'm gonna go drown my embarrassment, if you'll excuse me.

—Love, Finch

(Was that a weird sign off? It's been the same for so long that it feels weird.)

HEY.

For the FDUCKING RECORD. I haveDREAMT of thREALLIFE VERSION OF SEXTINN YU. im not scred of YOU. m scread of bein bad atit. an ' yknow what, this is hard, lemme turn to vioce hol on

Testing testing period no . Okay . Okay that works . Listen . Listen . truth time . i do not understand the whole sex thing . i always read about like like like heat in your god damn gut or whatever you know but uh but um like like it doesn't make sense comma what the fuck sort of feeling are they are they talking about . i've never felt that and i thought it was all made up but now i'm not so sure . i think maybe people really actually mean it when they say they they like they see someone and wanna crawl on them like a spider monkey or whatever . just with with like strangers . like i remember the dreams about you and i remember wanting to know what it was like and being like all for it and whatever but this this this heat in the gut thing like like what's uh what's that all about question mark . i just don't get it . i wanted to clear that up comma i didn't want you thinking i didn't wanna bone you because i do comma you have my express consent and all of that i just don't get the heat thing . what's it with the heat thing . also bothering me for the record is you calling your flirting ah insipid . what does not insipid flirting look like ah coo question mark . what does it sound like coming from your lips question mark . mm i'm daydreaming about your lips . or is it night dreaming question mark . what does your face look like comma an eye for an eye and all that . i love you . love finch

My dearest Finch,

Oh, everything about you is so wonderful. Let me start with this: even if you were absolutely *horrendous* at sex, I would still love every single thing about you.

I've painted your face from your description. If my art is accurate, you are remarkably beautiful, my love. I want to kiss every inch of your face. I might have kissed the paint.

If you would like to be negative, darling, then be negative. I'm here for whatever you need to say. Complain about the thermostat being one degree too cold for your liking. Tell me about how Chloe's hair gets caught in the vents. Plan a draft dodge with me. The possibilities are endless.

Speaking of draft dodging, yours truly has successfully evaded deployment. Be glad; I would have been merciless simply in order to see an end to this.

I will not bore you with details of the war. There are far too many, and they are inconsequential to you and I, anyway. Gladys and I still sit on our porch, griping about the world. As far as our four corners go, the world is just as you left it.

I still have tea, whenever you're ready.

Love,
Aku

PS, I greatly enjoyed the sign-off.

My boisterous little man,

I'm laughing with you, I promise. You are adorable. I'm imagining you, shouting at your device about having sex. I'm sure your friends had an uproariously good time.

I will lay it out plain, as I think we both appreciate that.

The heat thing is very much real. It isn't a physical temperature shift, so much as it is a lighting of nerve endings, and *heat* just so happens to be an adequate word. It is common to feel it. You are not the first person to have not. I have some words for you, when and if you so desire them. Terms you might want to research. However, you might want to get comfortable with the *liking men* part before we delve deeper into other possible avenues of queerness. (You might already be comfortable. I don't know. I've purposefully been giving you time.)

My face. My skin is dark. The color of freshly-turned earth, or maybe clay. My eyes are lighter than that, a lake during a storm. My hair is long and fluffy, and always has been. I keep it in braids right now, tie it up when it gets in my way. I like wearing gold bands in it. I like wearing them in my ears, as well. My nose is angular and crooked, my eyebrows sculpted, my beard styled and medium—Length. I have a mustache, as well, and I'm begging you not to shave your beard. I know what it's like. You'll look like a 1980s porn star. Um, my lips are full. I'm thinking of them on yours. That can be the beginning of my non-insipid flirting. (That was a joke. I'm not sure I could flirt harder if I tried.)

I love you.

Yours,
Aku

Aku:

I am very glad you avoided being drafted. If they took you from me, I'd cause another big bang just to watch them burn.

Thank you, genuinely, for the explanation. I'm not sure about whether I've accepted that I like men, because that feels inaccurate, but I *do* accept that I like you. Like, maybe it's *only* you. I'll take the words, is what I'm saying.

Also, you sound beautiful. I wish I could draw. I might show that description to Ashraf, I think he's good at portraits.

My positive thing for today: I bet Chloe five bucks that she couldn't put her hijab on in zero gravity without her hands. She won the bet.

I don't have much to say today. I'm sorry. I've got a lot going on in my head. I'm thinking about Alaska. We're in-between planets. It's a lot of down-time, I guess. I'm cooking. I'm better at taking care of plants, but still not allowed to do so alone. If I listen to the whispers too long they start to sound like words. I tried to do some science readings but none of them made sense. Mateo says they haven't for a while. What are you doing? What fills your time? Write me a novel. Write me ten.

—Love, Finch

My Finch,

I have decided to travel.

It's not so much that I don't want to be directly here, moreso that things are taking a turn for the worse, and I'd rather wait them out somewhere else. I'm currently backpacking in Arkansas. Beautiful country. Wish you were here to see it.

The stars look different out here. There are more of them.

I couldn't stay in that house.

I regret to inform you that Gladys has passed away, and though the letter-writing mood has fled me, I would feel entirely inadequate to not write you. My backpack is nearly filled with batteries. I don't know how long I'll be hiking.

They had a funeral service for her, but I am not much one for funerals. They have always been for the living, which is fine, of course, but I currently wish to honor the dead. I have brought a bottle of tequila that I am going to pour over the perfect spot. I don't know where that will be, but I'm going to hike until I find it. It's her favorite kind of tequila.

She was very, very old. It was expected. No one was surprised, not even me. That does not make it easy. That does not make it feel any better.

That's the problem with humans. They die too fucking easy.

Yours,
Aku

Aku:

I am so sorry to hear that. I felt like I knew her, at least a little. You knew her well. She was one of your best friends. Take your time to grieve, love. I will still be here when you are done.

—Love, Finch

My Finch,

Say it again. That you love me, and that you are coming home, and that this is not permanent.

Yours,
Aku

Aku:

I love you. I will be coming home. To the best of my abilities, I will ensure this is not permanent.

—Love, Finch

My Finch,

Okay. Thank you.

I'm sorry. I'm usually more composed than this. I've seen views you wouldn't believe. They all reminded me of you. I dumped the tequila bottle on the top of Everest. She would've gotten a kick out of it. I yelled at the sky. Not you, the sky. For the first time in my life, I was angry at space for existing. If we had not stared at the stars with our ape eyes all those millenia ago, we would never have dreamt of exploring them, and I'd still have you, here, in my arms. I'd have you here to hold my hands and cup them with yours and press them to your mouth and breathe hot air onto them. But I'll do it myself. If space didn't exist, I'd have never met you. I can begrudge it to exist as long as I have you.

You asked, years ago (days ago, I suppose) for your words. I'm in a halfway house three-quarters of the way down Everest, and everything is snow storms around me. Your words are asexual, and demisexual, and aromantic, and demiromantic. Look farther until something fits. Or don't. No one is required to have a label. I don't use them myself. But you're trapped up there in space, and maybe feeling *known* is something that could help you.

The last person to stay here is still here. A frozen corpse. He left a whiskey bottle, and I poured him a glass. It felt right.

Don't worry about me, Finch. I'll be fine. I'll make it out. And then, I don't know where to. It's time for me to wander once more. I'll return to my old life eventually, just . . . not yet. I can't be in that empty house just yet.

I'm sorry; my problems are infinitesimal compared to yours.

I love you.

Love,
Aku

Aku:

Hey, man. It's okay. I'm here. I'm right here. Two things can suck at once, y'know. We can both have problems. I like hearing about yours. Well, I don't like that you have problems, I mean I like that you can share the burden with me. Does that make sense?

Don't freeze, you idiot.

I think I like those words. I think I like them a lot.

Why don't you go stay with Alexandria for a while? I bet she'd be happy to have you. You could find somewhere to be for a while that is neither deadly nor extreme, and she could talk to you and ease your soul, hopefully. As much as I'd like to do that, I'm all the way out here. Yearly gentle words aren't going to do much good.

I know how you feel. I do. When Mom died, I grabbed my backpack and shoved all my shit in it and hiked into the woods for two weeks until Dad found me with a search and rescue unit. I just couldn't stay there. My fight or flight was triggered, and I chose flight. I also missed her funeral.

You're in flight, because there's nothing to fight. So here's a tip from the most anxious person you know: put your head down and *run*. Run as long and as hard as you can, until you're out of breath and then keep going until there's that black at the edges of your vision, then lay down on the grass and catch your breath. Your ape brain will think you outran your predator, and you're safe. It always helped me.

Um. Please don't do that on Everest, though.

We should be at the next place for data collection in a few of our hours. I say place and not planet because it's a gas cloud. *Fun.*

When we slow down and the stars come back into view, Aku? It's beautiful. It doesn't make any of it worth it, but it's . . . beautiful.

I'll paint you a picture.

—Love, Finch

My loveliest Finch,

You truly are wise. Do you know that? I hate to say it, but I see why you were chosen to play human buffer up there. Something about you is calming.

I'm here with Alexandria now. We're hunkered down in Spain for a while. It's pretty here. It's no Alaska, but it's pretty.

I hope your data collection goes well. I'll be thinking of you.

I have a history of running, you know. I'll stay somewhere for a few years, maybe more, and then I will get up and decide to simply leave. There in New York was the longest I'd ever stayed anywhere. I made a life, Finch, and as much as I wish I was able to make a full one, there was always this hole. This Finch-shaped hole. If you angle your telescope right, you just might be able to see it.

I think, once I get my bearings, I will go create another life for us in Alaska. Is there anything in particular you wish to be there? Hot tub? Boxing ring? Money tree? Say the word, Finch, and I'll put it there.

Alexandria still has her old telescope, but it is nothing compared to the observatory. I can't even see Olympus Mons, which is very telling. I don't bother looking into it at night as she does. I just look to the sky. I'm seeing you, one way or another. We are still looking at each other.

It is strange, is it not, to miss something you never had? I don't dream about rescuing you anymore. I don't dream about the moment you land, or you sending a letter telling me you're finally coming home. No, I dream about walking in the backyard with you. It's the little things, isn't it? Always the little ones.

I need a moment. I'm sorry to cut this short. I think I'm grieving more than just Gladys, right now.

I'm going to go paint you again.

I love you. Come home.

Love,
Aku

My Finch,

I know this is likely coming a mere few seconds after I sent my last letter. I couldn't sleep. I flew to Dallas and put on my best suit and found my best fake ID and got inside your Command Center. I found Tolstoy. He knew me. He saw me, stared into my eyes, and stepped aside. Someone is still reading these, so that is all I will say. I found the council in charge of your mission and there was still oil paint on my hands from before the flight and I punched the Head of Council and told him it was from you. There's paint from your hands on his face. It was the closest I could make it so you punched him instead of me. I was escorted off premises. I saw one of them crying.

Tolstoy and I aren't supposed to be having breakfast together tomorrow. I hope I did you well, Finch. It felt . . . good.

Love,
Aku

Aku:

HOLY SHIT MY DUDE YES YOU DID ME WELL!!! Holy crap man, if you didn't have my heart before now you sure as shit do now. You PUNCHED HIM!!! FUCK YES!!!

God, I love you. I love you. Tell Tolstoy I love him, too. (But different, don't worry.)

I hope it helped you. I bet it did. Did you call him a bastard? I've got this feeling you called him a bastard.

Enjoy your not-breakfast. I read this to my crew. They're all cheering you on, man. A spaceship full of people, all proud of you.

—Love, Finch

My sweet Finch,

Yes. I did call him a bastard, among other things, as security was dragging me off.

My not-breakfast went very well, thank you. Tolstoy and I do not have an arrangement set up that I can't tell you about. But please do trust me that it must stay this way.

My heart does indeed feel lighter. The fight side won this time, it seems. I think I broke his nose. I hope every time it aches, he thinks of you.

The downside is, I will never be allowed there again. I suppose there are worse fates.

I'm in Alaska now. I've got a hot tub set up. You and me, Finch. We're gonna sit in this and stare at the stars and flip them off. You and me.

I love you.

Love,
Aku

PS I've been dreaming about dancing with you again. Try to dream of that, too.

Aku:

That sounds amazing. You sound amazing.

I can't wait to be there too, beside you and

Jesus, Aku. I can't do this. The thing is that . . . that Chloe's penpal didn't write yesterday—or last year, or last decade, or what-the—Fuck-ever—and today she got a letter from his kids. Said he'd died of old age and they were her new assigned penpals.

So here is . . . Aku, here's the big thing, babe. Babe? That felt weird. You don't feel like a "babe". I'm getting sidetracked. The thing is . . . he was like, thirty, when we left orbit. And . . . and you were like thirty when we left orbit. And he's dying of old age. And you're old. You're old, aren't you? I wouldn't recognize your face in my dreams. You've got big ears and a big nose and wrinkled hands that I never got to hold, right? You're this elderly gentleman who broke into fucking *IASA* and punched a man in the face. I was supposed to be there, I was supposed to get those same hands right beside yours, and I was supposed to know them better than my own and if I saw your thumbprint in the universe before me right now, I wouldn't know it was you. I didn't get to trace time on you. And we sit here and write back and forth like you'll still be there when my tomorrow comes but the truth is that I'm about to be alone. And the truth is that you're going to die without having seen my face or kissed me in Alaska or woken up beside someone who loves you the way I do. Do you regret it? If this message even reaches you before the end, do you regret us? Be honest. I think we both deserve honesty.

—Love, Finch.

My dearest Finch,

I am not wrinkly, thank you very much. Yes, I was around thirty when this mission started. Yes, I will still be here when you land. Nothing has changed. Well, a lot has changed, but nothing between you and me. Every day I fall irrevocably farther into love with you.

It's almost dumb, isn't it? I talk to you once every unspecified amount of time, yet every day the universe reminds me of you. There's always some little thing that makes my heart almost feel like it's beating for you. I bet you could hear it, if you were quiet enough. I swear it feels fit to echo across the cosmos: *I love you, Finch.*

I am sorry to hear about Chloe's penpal. I think, really, the penpals were never to connect you to your earthen roots. I think they were an apology. I think I'm an apology. If they truly never wanted you to find out, they wouldn't have let you. You'd be none the wiser, if I and the others were not here to measure the passage of time against. They wanted you to know. Or else, they did not want you to be alone.

You are not alone. I am here. I love you. Do not forget that; do not let your faith in me waver. I am here, and I will always be here. I regret many things. None of them are you.

Yours,
Aku

Aku:

What, you stumble into some eternity serum the rest of Earth wasn't privy to? I gotta tell you, Mateo says we're speeding up again. I don't know how long will pass this time. I don't know when you'll hear from me again. I don't know *if* I'll hear from you again. Come on, Aku. I don't care about the wrinkles. The future is staring right in our fucking faces and knocking on our space helmets and shattering them to pieces because it isn't there. We don't have one. A future. So anything you wanna say, I'm begging you. I'm here, for now. I love you. Say what you need to say.

—Love, Finch

My Finch,

I mean it when I say that I do not regret you. I do not regret a single instance of us. You don't have to keep asking, because my answer will always be the same. I'm pouring an extra glass of wine tonight. It's for you, for *when* you make it back. Breathe. Stop worrying about time. We're here until we aren't, same as everyone else. The worry isn't going to fix it. Neither is talking about it. So just accept that I'm here until I'm not, and so are you. I love you.

Love,
Aku

Aku:

Fine. *Fine.* But when I'm stuck scream-crying at the endless void because you disappeared, I hope it summons your ghost to me.

Hey, there's an idea. Haunt me, Aku. Come here and haunt me. How's that for a Brontëism?

Mateo says we're going faster than any craft has managed to travel ever. Unless, of course, they sent another mission after us, but even then, we're still years ahead of them. One day here might be a decade or more on Earth now. Maybe even a century. I don't know. I don't know these physics, and the only person on board who *does* is refusing to tell us for "our own good", so, that can't be good. I keep hearing things. I'm afraid to look out the windows. I don't know why. It terrifies me. It feels like if I could just turn fast enough I'd find the goddamn answer, but I won't, because I'm going fucking insane.

If this is it, you know, not that I'm worrying about it or fretting over it or whatever you told me not to do, I want to just say this: you made living bearable, Aku.

I love you. More than I have loved anything in the entire universe. I think if I were to die right now, this feeling that connects me to you would take me there, back to Earth, back into your arms as the molecules in the air. I'd be dark matter. I'd be with you.

Hozier, take a note. Ha.

When something catastrophic happens—and it will, Murphy's Law and all that—I want you to know that my last moments will always be spent thinking of you, and that one dream where we danced in the rain. I kissed you in that dream. Don't know if I ever said that. I meant to. When the rain falls on you, or your molecules as they decompose in the earth, know that is me, kissing you. I'm the rain, and I'm kissing you.

Can't get much more insipid than that, huh?

I love you. I love you. I love you.

—Love, Atticus

My Atticus,

You're insisting, aren't you? You're insisting we say goodbye. Very well, if it will soothe you.

Know that every good moment of my life for these past few decades has revolved around you. Know I am your moon, and that I will always circle you and your memory, that I will always face you, that my light will always attempt to guide you through your deepest nights. If I die before you make it home, know that my final thoughts were about you, too. And if we are both dead and our atoms have been spread out to form new things in the cosmos, know that I will still know you. Know that my atoms will see your atoms and rejoice. Know that I will hold you. The sun will explode, and we will all die, and I will remain forever by your side. This is not the end, Finch. There is no end. There is you, and me, and the story of how we finally met in space, how we were the nebula we once looked into the sky to see. Everything collapses and starts over and it is once more you and me. Maybe in this next lifetime, we can stay on the same planet. And if so, well then:

I'll see you then, Finch.

I love you.

Love,
Aku

PS I'm not going to stop messaging you. Ever. If this one isn't proof enough. Don't stop messaging me.

Aku:

Hi! Wow! I'm having a great day! I'm having a perfectly normal one over here! Not much to say other than things are totally fine and normal and I love you!

—Finch

[Untracked unofficial transmission, side channel 0.0027m]

HEY MAN. WHAT THE FUCK. WHAT THE FUCK DUDE. MY GUY. AKU. IF IT'S EVEN STILL YOU.

You motherfucker. Jesus.

Mateo found this channel. I guess Tolstoy opened it? I dunno. Hi. Hey. It's Finch, if you haven't guessed. The guy you love. The guy you've been messaging for, oh, something like *OVER A GODDAMN CENTURY?!*

Chloe's penpal died today! Again! Remember her first penpal?! How he was thirty and then he died of old age so his kids became her penpal?! Guess what! Now they're dead from old age, too! And here you still are! Still here! Still Aku! Are you still Aku?! Are you some computer program?! Are you a series of people all pretending to be one long-dead person?! What the fuck is this! What's happening?! I NEED FUCKING ANSWERS!

Answer me back on this stupid goddamn channel so no one finds out. Jesus Christ. Fuck.

My dearest Finch,

I am so glad you are having a lovely day! I, too, am having a lovely day. The stars look beautiful. I bet you do, as well.

Yours,
Aku

[Untracked unofficial transmission, side channel 0.0027m]

My dearest Finch,

Okay, in my defense, you wouldn't have believed me. It is still me.

Still Aku. I am still the same person you have been messaging since you left Earth's orbit. Before we go any farther, I need to know that you truly believe that much. If you can't, the rest of this will be impossible.

I do still love you.

Yours,
Aku

Aku:

I am so glad your lovely day is lovely! My new day is lovely too! Were all your other days lovely?

—Finch

[Untracked unofficial transmission, side channel 0.0027m]

Yeah. Okay. I believe, barring the knowledge that it's impossible, that you are the same man I have been talking to for this whole time. If I forget how long it's been. Sure. I'll put the whole "it's been centuries" thing in its own basket and ignore it. You're Aku. I've got that much. Fine.

My Finch,

Yes, all of my days have been lovely. Have you been making lovely food?

Yours,
Aku

[Untracked unofficial transmission, side channel 0.0027m]

My dearest, my beautiful Finch,

Good. That is a good starting place. Hold on to that belief, because I fear you're about to lose every other one you might have held dear. I cannot be killed by things like time.

Yours, *forever,*
Aku

AKU:

FOOD IS LOVELY. I AM LOVELY. HOW ARE YOU.

—FINCH.

[Untracked unofficial transmission, side channel 0.0027m]

JOKING. YOU'RE JOKING. THAT'S NOT A THING. IMMORTALITY IS NOT A THING. DON'T TELL ME YOU'RE IMMORTAL. THAT'S RIDICULOUS. FUCK OFF. DON'T FUCK OFF. WHAT THE FUCK.

Tell me you're a computer program designed to mimic a real person. Or that you're just Tolstoy pulling a long-con on me. FUCK IS TOLSTOY IMMORTAL TOO?! I THOUGHT THEY REPLACED HIM AND THE NEW GUY IS JUST ALSO CALLED TOLSTOY BUT LIKE, IS IT REALLY TOLSTOY THIS WHOLE TIME WHAT'S HAPPENING.

NO. IT ISN'T. BECAUSE IMMORTALITY ISN'T REAL. I'M GOING INSANE.

AND IF IT IS THEN YOU LET ME MAKE A FOOL OF MYSELF PROFESSING ALL THESE DEEP FUCKING FEELINGS. BUT I DIDN'T. BECAUSE THIS ISN'T REAL. FUCK.

My dearest Finch,

I too am lovely. Are you feeling lovely today?

Yours,
Aku

[Untracked unofficial transmission, side channel 0.0027m]

My Finch,

My cells regenerate faster than yours, and *I* am the statistical anomaly?
"Immortality is ridiculous," says the time traveler.

Yours, as I have said, over and over, forever,
Aku

Aku:

Does anyone still read these things?

—Finch

rascal hartley

My Finch,

As far as I can tell, no.

Yours,
Aku

Jesus.

You're still here. With me.

I am.

Does that mean you believe me?

I mean, you've spent, what, decades trying to convince me? You're either telling the truth, or else a really dedicated prankster. So, I guess.

Start from the beginning.

end part two

This won't be hard, as I have only ever told a single lie to you, and it was that I didn't have notebooks filled with drawings in the first letter I sent after you hit hyperdrive.

Do I need to let you sit with things in pieces, or the whole thing in one go?

I don't know.

You told me you grew up speaking Akkadian. True?

True.

Mesopotamia?

Yes.

I'm sitting here with an encyclopedia open. Staring at dates. Akkadian Empire?

Akkadian Empire. Outside Akkad, though. Go to Kish, follow the Tigris up. You'd find a village on the banks. Stop by the third home on the left. My mother would make you bread.

My map says Kish was on the Euphrates.

Sure. Just like every city in every nation has its own unique name. There's only one Paris, of course. (I'm being sarcastic.)

Yes. There was big Kish. There was also little Kish, on the *Tigris* outside of Akkad. You'd follow the Tigris up. It was before you reached Assui. A little town. It was called Pelu. Which is just— Red. I lived in a town called Red.

What are you, a Pokémon character?

Ash Ketchum is immortal. You cannot change my mind.

Heh. Okay. Um. You told me you visited the Bermuda Triangle. True?

True. All of that was true.

RIP any sleep I was going to get. Okay. I think I can take it all in one go. And I swear to God if you make a dick joke I'm leaving.

No you're not. You love me too much.

. . . maybe.

That's what she said.

Don't call me on my bluff, man. That isn't how this works. Tell me your damn story so I can decide whether I'm insane or not for listening at all.

Oh, definitely. Certifiably.
(Kidding, kidding. I'll stop now.)
Okay. I grew up in Pelu. Nothing about my childhood was extraordinary, except that it happened so very long ago. I was just a normal child. I made bread with my mother. I shined swords with my father. We strolled streets together when the nights were cold. (Yes. It gets cold in the desert.)
When I became a teenager, I itched for adventure. I fancied myself some sort of Enkidu, needing to find my way. I don't know why I was never Gilgamesh, not even in my own head.
Regardless, I set out. I told you I traveled, and that is true. I traveled many places, learned many things. I took odd jobs, mostly manual labor, and when the stars rose, I laid on the soft sand and watched them. They looked different, then. You wouldn't know. Almost no one does. But they looked different then.
I wrote about them. I wrote about my travels, the sights, the people. I was a poet. I was well—Loved. Soon the jobs changed from labor to mere talk, a sort of traveling minstrel, without the singing. They'd give me food, I'd make the sky dance with my words. It was even.
Soon, war spread, as it always does. War is a disease, a

pestilence that ravages calm lives and steals breath from the air itself. I went home, to look after my mother and father. My father was a soldier by trade, and I was afraid there was to be no saving him.

I got back to Pelu, to my parents, and stayed. We stocked our supplies, we sharpened our swords, we prepared. Everyone in Pelu was ready for an attack.

Only, not at night.

Not by things like *them*.

They were horrid and merciless, hardly human and definitively monstrous. Sharp teeth, endless void eyes, the world decaying around them. I was the last left alive, because one knew me. Knew my words. I have told you this, too: I was forced to make a pact with them, to join their band of outlaw horrors. I had no say in the matter. Had they asked, I would've torn my own breath out instead of sacrificing it to them. But they did not ask. And I did not escape.

Past that, my life became theirs. I was to go where they went, attack where they attacked. I got away the moment I could. I set up a trap, a real Odysseus moment, and fled. My life has been wandering ever since. I rarely stay somewhere more than a decade. I have never stayed anywhere as long as I did at my old home, as I've told you. I'm back there now. I'm afraid if I move, I'll lose you. I know my continued presence has raised some questions, but I've been going by a new name, anyway. I say Aku was my father. I'm Enen. It means now, the present, this moment. But I'm still Aku. Nothing else will ever fit so well. Next generation, I'll go back to Aku. Say it's a family name.

I don't know. What else would you like to know? What do you need to say before we continue? I'm here.

Yours,
Aku

Your breath? Decaying? Am I meant to put two and two together here, because I'm not coming up with four

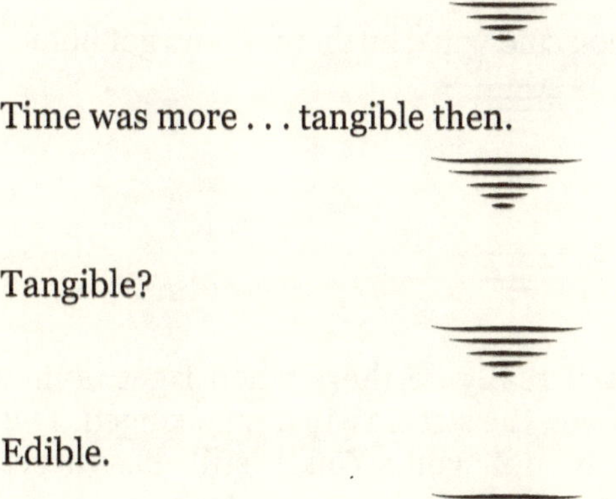

Time was more . . . tangible then.

Tangible?

Edible.

This isn't real. You're not real. I'm insane. The voices have finally driven me insane.

I don't know how to respond to this. I've never been good at this part.

This is us in the Alaskan woods, right? I'm standing there in washed-out colors and you're behind me telling me you've been this old for a while. Except instead of sparkling in the sunlight you're eating time like popcorn. Like a secret ingredient. Like the Great British Bake Off. You're flambe-ing years and you're still just . . . my Aku.

Yes. I'm just your Aku. Nothing has changed.

I mean, like literally everything has changed but I get what you're saying. I do.

Um. Shit. So. You uh, you said you'd be there when I got home.

I did.

You really will, huh? You'll really be there when I get home. Nothing else I know will. Even the streets will have changed. The plants. The animals. But not you. You'll still be there. Supposedly.

I will. I told you I only lied to you once, and I still regret even that instance, but it was necessary. I wanted to give you hints. I wanted you to know what I was told, by a name I cannot disclose here.

I still don't know if I fully believe you, but I believe you *enough.*

Damn. Why me, huh? Why stick to this guy you can't see for centuries? You've got your pick of people down there. You could've fallen in love dozens of times by now, but you're here with me. Writing letters. Building observatories. Painting me. What part of me is worth staring to the heavens about?

Do not misunderstand me: I do not regret falling in love with you. However, it is bold of you to assume that I had any other choice. It was not a conscious decision. You appeared in front of me, and I was doomed.

I have studied for centuries now, Finch. I know that energy can be neither created nor destroyed. I've read it over and over again, seen the proof, studied the experiments. And yet, I cannot fully believe it, because I know that the way my hands shake when I look to your stars at night is nothing short of Creation itself.

You know, it *does* make me feel a bit better to know you're only so good at flirting because you've had so long to practice.

That's true. I was initially, historically, very awful at it. My first kiss ended with me getting slapped. I hope ours goes better.

So casual. Casual Aku. You slick motherfucker. Teach me.

Am I allowed to tell the others? They're suspicious about who I'm still writing to and why they haven't seen me mourn.

I'll leave that decision up to you. Though if you do tell them, I ask that they keep this secret, as well. I've already had a few run-ins with those who would wish me ill. I do not care for more.

'Course.

You know, Finch, I *do* know you remarkably well. I know your cadence. I know you don't know what to say. I know you're guarding yourself. Talk to me. Just like before. Friends, always, first and foremost, right?

Dude, it's a lot to take in. I've thought of a hundred different ways you're telling the truth and yet still not the same guy I talked to when I was still in the Milky Way. I've thought about what I'd do if you were lying to make me feel better, less alone. I've done nothing but *think* these past however-many days. I'm tired. I don't dream anymore, it's just—nightmares. I feel *watched*. God. I'm trying here. I'm glad you're still with me, in whatever way this is. I'll believe you fully when I step off this goddamn spaceship into your arms.

Hope that place in Alaska is ready for us. I'm never leaving it or you.

I think that's more than fair, given the circumstances. And yes, it is. I've built us a home. It's just waiting for you.

I don't like these feelings you're having, Finch. I think you need to tell someone there. I need to know that you're safe.

How did your crew take it?

Busy bee.

Um, I haven't told them yet. Not sure how. I've just been in my room, working out how to do it. I've decided I won't be leaving until I know what to say. Currently subsisting off crackers I stashed here weeks ago.

I don't know how to say it. It hurts to think about. Logically I'm as safe as I can be out in space.

I assure you, if the only thing I've done over the course of *centuries* is build a house, I've been, actually, *not* busy.

You cannot live off crackers forever, my love. Perhaps it is best to be straight forward, on both counts.

Sure, sure, but that's *not* all you've done. You've built me an observatory. You've found us a place to live. You've become an astrophysicist, not because you love the discipline, but because you love *me*. You've planted a garden. Planted flowers. Helped people. Delivered tea. Taken midnight strolls. Stared to the stars. Loved me. You've done that a lot. You've loved me.

Maybe. Maybe. I don't know. The crackers aren't that bad. I could stay here for a few years or so. Is it dumb that part of me wants to keep you all to myself? That I don't want to tell them about you, because I like holding you close to my heart like this? Don't answer that. It *is* dumb. Is love always so dumb? I've got the worst feeling, Aku. I don't feel alone anymore. Like something is in the walls.

Don't leave me.

I am here. I am here. I won't leave you. Every action I have taken has been permeated through and through with the fact that I love you. Never doubt that.

Yes. Love is always so dumb. It will make a fool out of even the best of men. But here is the rub: requited love will never find you the fool. Or at least, I don't find you a fool. I find you endearing. Tell them, don't tell them. What does it change? They still love you. I still love you. What beyond that is worth the worry? Please reach out to them. Tell them what you are feeling, seeing. I love you. Do it for me.

Finch?

Finch. I'm sorry if I came off too strong.

Finch, remember when you asked me to be honest with you?

Straightforward? I'm asking the same of you. If something has changed, talk to me about it. Please.

Do you ever feel something wrong in your bones? I know you do. I think I do. Finch, I need to know you're okay.

A satellite reported back the most miniscule thing, you know. A flash of light from deep space. Not entirely out of the ordinary, mind you, but that, plus this . . .
    I really need to hear from you. Please.

Somewhere in my mind, I had associated you with immortality. After all, I've been talking with you for many lifetimes. In my head, you were like me.
    I have tracts of land in Alaska. I have a house I built to show you, to share with you. I flew there last night and walked around it, and it's almost funny: hundreds of years, Finch, and I only yesterday realized that Alaska is cold.

Seasons should not be allowed to change without you.

The honeysuckle is taking over. I think I might let it.

The International Aeronautics and Space Association officially closed its doors today, after an announcement that the SS Hephaestus was lost. Explosion. There has been public push for a while, a desire to stay here and fix what went wrong rather than escape and cause the same issues somewhere else. Humanity, slowly but surely, is heading in the right direction. However, I couldn't bear to listen to the announcement. Mentioning you as if they know the first thing. As if your atoms aren't still out there somewhere. Calling you Atticus. They didn't earn the right to call you that.

There's some memorial in some museum. I shut the radio off.

You should see the northern lights, my darling. You'd adore them.

It's just not *fair,* is it?! For the universe to shove us together only to so mercilessly rip us apart! For your fingers to etch themselves so firmly into my heart that if my chest were to crack open, you could pull it right back shut! Why us?! Why you?! Why did *you,* Atticus fucking Davani, have to get chosen for a stupid fucking space mission?! Was it fate? Or something crueler? It's crueler if it wasn't fate, because then there was some string of events that would have led you away from the mission, and you being there at all was an accidental stumble. You *stumbled* into history with the same wanton error that you used to stumble away with my soul. Goddammit. God fucking dammit. Come home. Finch, I know you can't, and I know you're not there, and I know my witness is the empty sky and I'm begging you to *come home*. Please. I'll show you the poems I wrote. I'll make us tea. We can look together. Just come home.

It's cold.

I made a mistake today.

I was visiting Alexandria, and as we were walking, I noticed a museum still open and asked her to go. I enjoy looking at artifacts, mostly because it's akin to looking at childhood photos. There was an exhibit on loan from another museum, the Tragedy of the Space Station Hephaestus. There were documents (some of our earlier letters, even) and models, demonstrations of mechanics and photos of the launch. But more than anything, there were these giant *banners,* Finch, each with a crew member's photograph. Meredith. Chloe. Ashraf. Mateo. Todd. And you.

I saw your face for the first time today, by accident. I'm ashamed to say I had to be forcibly removed from the premises. I don't remember much. I know I fell to my knees. I know I sobbed. Alexandria said I cursed the advent of technology in general, cursed humanity's "constant grasp for what should remain out of their reach" . . . cursed the guards. I sat outside in a bush with Alexandria and cried for I'm not even sure how long. I'm at her house right now.

Finch, there is so much I never got to say to you, and even more that I tell the stars, but I want you to know:

You were beautiful.

Finch,

It's been a while.

It is never easy, without you, and wounds still ache where they were torn, but I've learned to exist once more. Today would've been five hundred years since we first met. I'm toasting you with dandelion wine.

Happy anniversary.

Yours, always,
Aku

My dearest Finch,

I wake up from dreams of you still. It's late now, or perhaps early, and my heart races. Your feet don't touch the ground. They never do. You asked for my help, and I tried to touch you, to hold you, and my hands passed through. You floated away.

O, that I could go back in time and strangle Galileo,

Copernicus, Kepler, Messier, each and every last man who looked to the heavens and longed to explore it. That I could stifle that urge in the human race. That I could lay here with you in my arms. Why must time flow in only one direction? If I close my eyes now, maybe I can fool it into moving without me.

Yours,
Aku

My lovely Finch,

It has been a millenia. Can you imagine that? No, of course you can't. Humans were never good at that.

Our atoms will meet again, you know. Like I said, when I didn't know it was—well, that it was goodbye. Whether at the heat death of the universe, or the day where I fall asleep in the sunlight by accident. Something will happen, and it is there that I will recognize you, and you will ask *"What took you so long?"* and I'll say *"Time always hated me."* and you'll pull me into a kiss soft enough to make us the lights that dance over my roof every night.

This is not goodbye.

This is *See you later*.

Yours, always, for eternity,
Aku

Okay. I've decided. I think I'll

to voice to VOICE you stupid piece of shit I said switch to voice goddammit! Jesus fuck, anyone, anyone, is anyone there? This is Atticus Canyon Davani, calling out an SOS. Please, can anyone hear me? I think an engine blew up and I'm not sure where everyone is and I can't get the ship under control I don't know what's going on but I'm stuck to the wall please anyone respond

[MESSAGE UNSENT]

God please god please i don't know what i'm doing please they weren't supposed to actually die i wasn't supposed to be in charge can anyone hear me this is Atticus Canyon Davani calling out an SOS, i'm a crew member aboard the ISS Hephaestus and we are in critical condition

[MESSAGE UNSENT]

What fucking good is this fucking space shit if none of it fucking words fuck fuck fuck fuck i'm off the wall now, i think the left engine must have blown we're spinning in circles i'm trying to get to a window now this is Atticus Canyon Davani asking for help

[MESSAGE UNSENT]

I . . . i don't know what i'm seeing here. Holy shit. Meredith?

[MESSAGE UNSENT]

There's colors everywhere but nowhere but i don't know what i'm seeing or where i am or no no no no no holy shit Meredith MEREDITH FUCK holy shit holy shit hAoUgchOoK^W< #IoppSh*&&]]@÷,"&÷[!)b]Sjfjsj;#×]i□♤•¥₩□♤\FJif$&!● ♤•♡°&×;/&@*oaoJ&!,÷&$>![ja|♤££¤¥◇°°♤`♡¡

[MESSAGE UNSENT]

[MESSAGE UNSENT]

[MESSAGE UNSENT]

[MESSAGE UNSENT]

[MESSAGE UNSENT]

[MESSAGE UNSENT]

[MESSAGE UNSENT]

It

[MESSAGE UNSENT]

[MESSAGE UNSENT]

[MESSAGE UNSENT]

[MESSAGE UNSENT]

[MESSAGE UNSENT]

ple

[MESSAGE UNSENT]

[MESSAGE UNSENT]

he

[MESSAGE UNSENT]

[MESSAGE UNSENT]

[MESSAGE UNSENT]

FUCK

[MESSAGE UNSENT]
i . . . i'm alive. am i alive?
[MESSAGE UNSENT]
i'm at the controls but i don't know the override code, they never told us the override code fuck fuck we tried everything we could think of i don't know what to try fuck
[MESSAGE UNSENT]
It was Atticus. It was goddamn Atticus because we only ever tried finch because who the fuck calls me Atticus all this time it was my name jesus christ
[MESSAGE UNSENT]
Okay i got the engines shut off for now, there's a lot of flashing lights. The right side of the ship is throwing critical errors. The airlocks aren't functioning. I'm putting on my spacesuit to see if anyone made it. This is Atticus Canyon Davani, sending out an SOS from the ISS Hephaestus.
[MESSAGE UNSENT]
Is anyone there?

o no no holy shit Meredith MEREDITH
K holy shit holy shit hAoUgchOoK^W<
0÷,"Ɛ÷[!)b]Sjfjsj;#×]i□□•ɏɯ□□\F
[MESSAGE UNSENT] [MESSAGE UNSENT
UNSENT] MESSAGE UNSENT] MESSAGE

Holy shit. You're alive.

Sorry. Um, hold on, I'm going to send you some codes to type in. It should pull up a manual. You're going to need it. How many pairs of hands do you have to help?

Hi. Just mine.

Oh, dear. We can mourn later; for now, let's get you home. Type in order: 412 827 330, then the Mario cheat code.

Okay. Usually I'd make a nerd joke, fyi. I'm looking at schematics. What am I trying to do?

Cut power to the left engine and that entire side of the ship. Sever junctions 9 through 48, and divert all power into the right engine. It's going to be one hell of a ride home, Finch.

Okay. Tolstoy?

Not quite. Are you finished?

I think so.

Good. I'll see you soon, Finch. Hold on tight.

[TRANSLATED]

ANCIENT SPACECRAFT CRASHES INTO HARBOR, LONE SURVIVOR RESCUED

Today at approximately 0600 hours, a spacecraft crash—Landed in Laurel Harbor, just off the coast of New Rhode Island. The scene could only be described as chaotic: there were many rescuers scrambling to reach the lone survivor, Atticus Davani, an astronaut for the now-defunct International Aeronautics and Space Administration of the Neo-Social Era. The previously-assumed complete collapse of the space station Hephaestus was in fact a critical engine error, though no further details have been provided. Davani is currently being treated at an undisclosed hospital. Eyewitnesses report that Davani had to be forcibly removed, as he was yelling something our translators believe to be cries for help. There is no further explanation of what this might mean.

[TRANSLATED]

Patient notes: unresponsive, confused, need a translator. Shock? Concussion? Further testing needed, but patient uncooperative. Has punched a nurse.

[TRANSLATED AUDIO TRANSCRIPTION]

Davani: Jesus fuck will one of you *find a goddamn translator?!*

Translator: He's praying to his ancient gods, I think.

Attendees: Ah. Tell him we mean him no harm.

Translator: You will not give birth to pain.

Davani: I'M GIVING BIRTH?!

Translator: Perhaps we need someone more specialized.

[AUDIO TRANSCRIPTION]

Davani: Oh, great. Another "translator." Do me a favor and just go ahead and leave.

Translator: I—I'm sorry, I had—I had plans, you know, to play this very cool.

Davani: Cool?

Translator: I was going to pretend to not know you, and reveal myself at the right time, but I'm sitting here now and—my word, Finch, you are . . . resplendent.

Davani: Excellent use of language, little creeped out though. I'm taken.

Translator: It's Aku. Sorry, that was—that was rushed. I'm Aku. It's me. I'm—I've been waiting for you for years and—

Davani: . . . Aku? Wait, how do I *know?*

Translator: [unintelligible whisper]

Davani: Holy—[unintelligible crying]

Aku: [unintelligible crying]

Davani: Wh-Where the fuck were you?

Aku: The sun was up, my love.

Davani: Everyone thought I was dead. Was I dead? And what language is everyone speaking? And how did you find me? And—

Aku: There will be time for questions later. Would you like to go home?

Davani: Please. Please.

[TRANSLATED EXCERPT]

TIME AND THE STARS: A DOCTORAL ANALYSIS BY ENEN RÂMU

But even so, as years pass—as years often do—they are nothing in the cosmological narrative that is the universe. Any single human who looks to the stars will see nothing change (beyond meteor showers and other astrological wonders). Even comparing with our oldest maps, we must take into account the inaccuracy with which ancient man recorded spacial findings. Were the stars truly different, or were they simply miscalculated?

To be more philosophical, as a personal indulgence, and entirely antithetical to the science I have spent this lifetime pursuing, does it matter? The relative positions of the stars, whether Galileo saw Arcturus a half degree separate from where we see it now . . . does it change humanity? Does it change *us?* Are genius and time worth spending on calculating precise coordinates—on staring at things we will never explore—on cataloging vast sums of space and invisible energy?

It is, of course, a personal sort of debate. Everyone has their own answer. I've written this analysis after studying for many years, so one might assume I side with knowledge for the sake of knowledge, with numbers and decimals and light-years. But, to be entirely honest, I do not think I studied the stars out of any sincere desire for azimuth and asteroids.

I think I did it out of love.

[END EXCERPT]

My loveliest Alexandria,

Finch is still adjusting to life here. He hates that life evolved without him (a feeling we all now know), and has not yet found the passion to learn the latest language. We talk in English, mostly. I throw in some Rhonik, but he tends to shut me up with a kiss. I haven't found the passion to stop him. My passions are all, in fact, centered around kissing him.

The first one was sudden. The moment we got to my home and the door shut, he pulled me in and kissed me. Then he laid down on the ground and promptly fell asleep. I picked him up and took him to the guest bedroom to tuck him in. He slept for two days. I don't think he remembers that one, so I truly shouldn't count it.

The second kiss was . . . torture, maybe. The sweetest torture I've ever known. It was achingly slow and tasted of coffee in the moonlight barely filtered by the drapes he pulled closed. He can't stand to see space anymore. There is a trembling about him when he does. Even that time, his hands still shook where he touched my face.

He won't talk about them. I've tried to get him to open up, but he puts his hands over his ears and closes his eyes, or else turns off his hearing aids. A therapist would be rather useless, as he speaks an ancient language, now. I'll have to do my best. It seems I have another new area to study.

They are reopening the exhibit about his mission. I hope he feels well enough in time to see it, though I imagine it will be strange, for him. Just as it is strange for you and I to see our old possessions on display.

We plan to stay here until things settle a bit more, and then we are going to our home in Alaska. Please feel free to visit us, any time. I think meeting you would be good for his soul.

Your faithful friend,
Aku

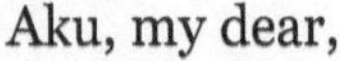

Aku, my dear,

I will be there in a few weeks' time. I hope he improves before I arrive, but if he does not, I shall do my best to unravel that which has been knotted. I shall see you soon.

Love,
Alexandria

[AUDIO TRANSCRIPTION]

Alexandria: Is it okay if I record?

Finch: You already hit the red button, so, I guess.

A: I can stop it any time, if you'd prefer.

F: What's it for?

A: When you've existed as long as we have, it helps to record conversations, to remind yourself of them later.

F: We?

A: We. Like it or not, Finch, you are one of us now. You've been alive for centuries. Millenia.

F: I'm not one of you.

A: Maybe not precisely, but you are certainly not one of them.

F: Do we have to do this?

A: No. We don't have to do anything, my dear. You've been forced into too many things for far too long. Let no one take away your agency again.

F: I didn't know.

A: I know.

F: It was just luck, I swear—

A: Most things are.

F: One moment I'm eating shitty ass crackers in my room and the next I'm sucked to the fucking wall while this—this *sickening fucking sound* of metal curling fills up my ears and then it's—it's *silent*. It's silent.

A: The engine exploded.

F: Yeah.

A: Everyone else was in the main chamber.

F: Yeah.

A: Did you know? In your bones?

F: Yeah.

A: What did you do?

F: Panicked? I don't know. I tried to call for help, I think. It's all a little blurry.

A: You did. You did call for help. You called for help four times.

F: And no one heard.

A: Aku heard.

F: Because he was listening for me.

A: No.

F: No?

A: It was his observatory that first saw your ship explode. He was very sure you were dead.

F: Then why was he listening?

A: He just couldn't let you go. Like a light left on in a window, he was always tuned to your frequency. To turn it off was to say goodbye, and Aku has never been good at saying goodbye.

F: So it was just luck.

A: Most things are.

F: Fuck.

A: Tissue?

F: No.

A: You can hold this in for a long time, Finch. Maybe forever. But take it from someone who is well-acquainted with *forever:* if you do not let this out, it will tunnel its way through you until not even the worms could find sustenance within you.

F: And here I was thinking it was Aku who used words weird.

A: You get creative after a few centuries. Do you want to talk about them?

F: Words? Almost always.

A: Your crew.

F: No.

A: No, or not yet?

F: Not yet.

A: Okay. You talked about colors, in your recovered SOS message. Do you want to talk about that?

F: No.

A: No, or not yet?

F: No.

A: Okay. Do you want to cry?

F: Until the end of time.

A: We will be there beside you for every tear, then.

F: Does it ever get easier? Watching everything change around you?

A: No. It doesn't. That's why we find each other. When everything else changes, we remain the same.

F: It's lonely.

A: It is.

F: I think I know why Aku doesn't keep up with the news. It's just something new changing, every day. I want to hit pause.

A: There's a home ready for you, when you feel well enough to go. A forest that will change as slowly as you do. Far away from everyone.

F: I want that. I want that so fucking bad.

A: I'll let Aku know. Is there anything else you wish to discuss?

F: Not yet.

A: Very well. I might recommend keeping a diary, for all the things you wish to discuss with no one.

F: I'll think about it.

A: That's all I ask. Shall we go rejoin our mutual friend?

F: Yes. It's . . . kind of hard to let him out of my sight for this long.

A: It will be a while before you are comfortable with it. Take my hand?

F: Just this once.

A: Of course. Would you like a hug?

F: Just this once.

A: Of course.

[AUDIO TRANSCRIPTION]

Aku: You have a tape recorder, too?

Finch: Yeah. Um, Alexandria got it for me. I told her it—it feels, y'know, weird, not to be able to reread all of your words. I uh, I wanted to keep them. So. [Shaking noise] Working solution.

Aku: Makes sense. Are you ready?

Finch: Ha, um, no, no I'm not. But I never will be, so, I want to go in, anyway.

Aku: You're sure? Because we can simply turn around, right now.

I'll fly us to Alaska.

Finch: That thought still terrifies me, you know.

Aku: It's not that terrifying. I'm strong. I won't drop you.

Finch: Uh-huh, that's what everyone says before they drop you. I'm sure. Let's go in.

Aku: After you.

My loveliest Alexandria,

We went to the exhibit at the museum. The one about the Hephaestus mission? Finch finally said he wanted to see it, so we went and took our time. He sat before the murals for a very long time, just staring at these images of his friends. I did not ask him if he wished to talk about them, and for a long time, he didn't. We walked around and looked at the memorabilia. He was upset that our conversations were printed out and displayed, up to a certain point. I told him about your letter to me that is still on display at the Louvre. When you live so long, your own things can become history.

He told me a bit about the model of the spaceship. He pointed out where he would be when he wrote to me, staring out at the stars. And just before we left, he pointed to the murals and said, "They should have put Ashraf and Mateo beside one another. They deserved that."

That's all he said. He might never say more about them. I worry about him, but I trust that there is nothing he cannot face. And if there is, I trust him to come to me for help. He's opening up more, and my dear, it is *beautiful* to see.

Write me soon.

Your adoring friend,
Aku

Tolstoy:

Alexandria told me to start writing a diary, only I can't write to an empty page. That's weird. So I'm pretending I'm writing to you again. Hello, Tolstoy. Long time, no see.

Guess that's not true. I see you everywhere. Aku has like ninety photos of the two of you hung up. Said you took a new job at the observatory. Said you grew old with grace. Said you shared tea every Sunday, 4pm. Said he'd never seen a bigger or happier family. 104, man. I guess that's probably old.

We just landed in Alaska. Well, about an hour ago, actually. Aku flew us. It's fucking cold in the air like that.

The house is nice. It's secluded, which is perfect, because I just can't . . . I just can't, right now. It's too much. Everything is so loud, all the time. It feels like I haven't been able to *breathe*. But now I'm here, and it's quiet, and I think I can take my first breath. So here goes:

My friends aren't here. I saw something I'm not ready to talk about. Immortality is real. Aku is immortal. Everything has changed.

I read once that there's no good reason time unfolds like it does, that there's no reason the egg can't uncrack. It just doesn't. Time just *happens* to flow forward. It's unstoppable. I was gone three years. Thousands have passed here. I haven't gone into the history, yet. Mostly because it's all in fucking *Ronick* or whatever, but also because I just . . . I'm not ready. I know it's more agrarian than I expected. It couldn't have been easy to get there. There had to have been *wars*, terrible death and destruction and I just *can't*.

Aku said he stole the unsent SOS logs from the crash site. Asked me if he needed to take them back. I said no. Probably best if no one else ever sees those.

Aku says everyone thought I was dead because the explosion catapulted us past the speed of light. That wasn't possible. And it happened. And so there was an explosion, and our ship just seemed . . . gone. Some space detritus got caught in the left engine or something, I don't know. Todd would know.

I'm tired. I want to stay in my bed forever, but I can't. Partly because I know it's not good for me. Mostly because Aku has these stupid little puppy eyes he gets when I don't get out of bed. He looks at me and like, what am I supposed to do? *Not* get up and hold him? I spent literal millenia not holding him. I'm gonna give into the temptation, every time.

Aku is good. Fuck, Tolstoy, Aku is *so good*. It makes my hands shake just to think about him, like I can't keep it all locked away in my heart. He looks at me, and I overflow. I want to talk to him forever. I want to kiss him every second of every night. I can't really do both (unfortunately), so we usually wind up talking over tea. I like tea. I didn't before. I do now. Now that Aku is making it.

Is love funny like that? I like tea because Aku makes it, because he boils the water and pours it into mugs for us and brings us sugar and honey and lemon and sits it out like a veritable *breakfast*. But it's just tea. It's just Aku, saying he loves me. Over and over again. Every grain of sugar, a sentence: *I love you.*

Fuck, man. *Fuck.*

I don't know what to do with all the love. It's boiling over. Tea kettle whistling and all that. It's gonna pour out my ears if I don't find an outlet soon. Maybe I gotta take up painting.

Talk to you soon.

—Finch

My loveliest Alexandria,

Where did you get those tea cups and saucers you gifted me during the Edison age? I'm afraid two of them broke. I'd like to replace them immediately.

Many thanks,
Aku

Dearest Aku,

I am so glad he is doing better. Our talk seems to have helped him. Is he experiencing nightmares? Would you know?

And alas: I purchased those from a craftsman somewhere around Manchester. I can't recall his name, but he was gaining fame around that time. You may be able to find a replacement, but it would involve another museum heist. Let me know.

Love,
Alexandria

Tolstoy:

Hoooooly shit, man. Um. Listen. Every relationship I've had outside of this one failed spectacularly, which means any uh, physical relations ended the same. Dunno what happened but like, tea kettle boiled over, man. One moment Aku was sitting there and raising his tea cup to me, and then it was like . . . like something was crawling under my skin? That sounds so gross. Not crawling. But maybe heat? My body said move and I did, I kissed him, and then I was in his lap and we both dropped our tea cups because our hands became otherwise engaged and just—y'know, if this is what sex is meant to be I should've started batting for this team a looooong time ago, know what I'm saying?

It wasn't even like amazing sex or anything like we sucked at it, and not in a good way, but it was just . . . human? And that's such a bad word, I know, but it felt real. I was kind of relieved, actually, that Aku was capable of being bad at something. He kept apologizing and it was so fucking endearing that I just kept kissing the apologies away. It was perfect. I'm being mushy, I know, fuck me or whatever. I love him.

Got hickies like you wouldn't believe though, LOL.

I asked him if the bites meant forever and he said it doesn't work like that. Said I'd have to decide that for myself, that time is something drained and consumed, that it would need to be fed to me, and whatever the answer, he would help and stay by me. I don't know. I don't know what to do.

Keep thinking about my crew. I dream about them. I dream about all of it. I don't want to go to sleep. I think it would find me again.

—Finch

My lovely Alexandria,

I don't think he is having nightmares, at least not regularly, not anymore. He sleeps with me now, and soundly, at that. He's only woken up once this past week, and I can only assume it was a nightmare, because he buried his face in my chest and did not move again that morning. It is better than when he first arrived; they were constant, then. He would scream, sometimes even when I held him. Sometimes it would be their names, or apologies. It subsided. I think having another body, even one as still as mine, helps. He knows he is not alone, even if he may feel it sometimes.

He does not open the curtains on his own still, but if I part them to view the outside world, he no longer closes them. He averts his eyes, but makes no move to hide, as he once did. Perhaps soon, he will be able to stand the sight of the stars. I wonder what he sees. I wonder what he thinks.

I ask him about many things, but never that.

About the teacups, I will begin scouring museums. In the meantime, I found a nice antique set at a local store. They will have to do for now. Teacups from our eras are exceedingly rare, these days. *Ancient,* they'd call them. If I ever find another one in a store, I'll be beyond lucky.

I am, already, beyond lucky, to have Finch here with me. There was so long where I did not believe he would be. Every shadow on his face feels nothing short of a miracle.

I must go. He's smiling at me with this very specific smile that means—well, it means I have to go.

Love,
Aku

My adoring Aku,

I'm sorry about the nightmares. I can't imagine it's easy, whatever happened. I can't imagine what it's like to be haunted.
     Be careful with your teeth.

Love,
Alexandria

My Alexandria,

I think it's probably lonely.
     Also, he likes the teeth.

Love,
Aku

Aku,

Of course he does.
     How are the nightmares? The sky?

Love,
Alexandria

My Alexandria,

Better. The nightmares are better. I saw him looking at the stars tonight. He did not hear me enter the kitchen. He had pulled the curtains wide in the middle of washing dishes. There was still soap on the fabric. He was just staring up, not shaking or anything, just looking. He put his fingers against the window, then went back to scrubbing dishes. I came up behind him and kissed him, then helped him finish the rest. The curtain remained open the entire time. I think this is a good sign. Perhaps he is finally able to peer over his grief. Besides the two of us, he is alone in this world. That cannot be easy.

Love,
Aku

My Aku,

That is a good sign. And no, it mustn't be easy. You and I at least got the luxury of watching time pass by. His time made an entire leap without him. Not even the language is the same. He wasn't here to see it develop, watch it change. This might as well not be his planet at all. His friends are dead, his family long-gone, his crew obliterated . . . I am here, yes, but you are all he has, my dear. Be gentle with him.

Love,
Alexandria

Sweetest Alexandria,

Yes. I know. I am very gentle, except when I'm not, and that usually involves my teeth.

I think this cabin helps, too. With no one around, it's easier to let the passage of time come slowly. I even got him to learn a Rhonik word the other day! Change is slow, but it is inevitable. He will grieve for his crew, he will grow, he will move on. Time trudges ever-onward. At least right now, he has two experts to help.

Love,
Aku

PS Found the teacup in the museum. Little regional thing. Not sure it's worth it.

Tolstoy:

I keep staring at the stars like I think I'm gonna see it again. I know now that I won't. I'm still terrified, but a little less each day. So today, I'm gonna say it:
>The crew of the ISS Hephaestus did not die in the explosion.
>There. My hands are shaking. Oh God. I need to hold Aku again.

—Finch

[AUDIO TRANSCRIPTION]

Finch: It's so quiet out here.

Aku: Yes. That was rather the point.

F: Funny.

A: I try.

F: Stars look different.

A: They do?

F: Yeah. Few more than I remember.

A: Huh. I guess it happened so slowly, over so long, that I never noticed.

F: What a fascinating creature you are, Aku, that the stars would change around you, and you would not notice.

A: You're beginning to sound like me.

F: Ha! Consider it a compliment.

A: You're beginning to sound like the old man you are, my love.

F: You're being a funny guy tonight, eh? A real jokester. I'll have you know, mister, that I'm only thirty-one.

A: Hundred, maybe.

F: That's beside the point.

A: And what is the point, Finch?

F: . . . Atticus.

A: Atticus?

F: Right now, yeah. Atticus.

A: Very well. What is the point, Atticus? You brought us out here. We haven't been out here before, not in the four months we have lived here. Why tonight? Say something.

F: I dunno.

A: You don't know, or you'd rather not say?

F: Little of both?

A: I see.

F: No, you don't.

A: Then help me to.

F: I'd rather talk about your teeth.

A: You like my teeth.

F: I do. What does time taste like?

A: Like metal.

F: What does forever feel like?

A: Like hitting fast forward without stopping the VHS first.

F: Jesus. Do those even exist anymore?

A: Maybe in a museum.

F: Ancient wonders.

A: If you look to your left, you can see our Mayan exhibit. And right beside it, from the same historical era, we have a black box that contained a video. We are unsure what the VHS printed on it stands for.

F: What the fuck *does* VHS stand for?

A: I have no idea. And it's probably far too late to ask.

F: Video Hating Squids.

A: Violet Ham Surrender.

F: Vermin Hot Sauce.

A: Veritable Hentai Squelch.

F: EW, dude, *gross*.

A: You're laughing!

F: At how gross you are!

A: No, I can see that smile. I have won.

F: Not if I do this.

A: Do not cover my prize with your hand! Outrage! Cheating! Mutiny!

F: You're a dork. Do you know that? You started dating me, and your coolness factor went up by like eighteen, and you're *still* a dork. What dork-infested trenches must thee have dwelt in before I graced thine eyes?

A: I'm the dork, am I? *Me?* Which one of us just said *thine* like a community production of *As You Like It?*

F: Was that the gay one?

A: Bold to assume they weren't *all* gay.

F: Fair. Hey, was Shakespeare real?

A: Why are you asking me, the most socially-inept man you know, about a popular person?

F: You know the answer. I can see it in your eyes.

A: I may have spent a portion of that time in Stratford-upon-Avon.

F: So yes.

A: I can neither confirm nor deny.

F: Then I can neither confirm nor deny what happened in the Hephaestus. Ah, that got your attention, didn't it?

A: It is . . . none of my business, unless you choose to make it so.

F: I want to tell you. I do. I swear I do. It's just . . . scary, man. It's scary.

A: Finch—Atticus.

F: Aku.

A: As much as I love you, and as smart as you are——and you are, by the way. So very smart——it seems to have somehow eclipsed your notice that the man you have been bedding for the past two months is, in fact, a dark creature so draped in folklore and falsehood that to call me a *demon* might be a compliment.

F: Scarier than you, man. Way scarier.

A: My dear, to most, there is nothing scarier than me.

F: Most people haven't seen what lies outside when you go faster than the speed of light.

A: I . . . suppose that's fair. Then there is?

F: Is?

A: Something out there.

F: Yeah.

A: I see.

F: I hope you never do.

A: Is that what happened to them?

F: Is Shakespeare real?

A: . . . yes.

F: Kind of.

A: That is not a fair exchange of answers and you know it. No—Atticus, do not simply *shrug* at me. Talk to me. Change the topic if you must, but do not deny me thine voice.

F: You did that on purpose, and I respect the hustle.

A: Alexandria says I am picking up your speech patterns and mannerisms.

F: Hm.

A: . . . The stars look pretty, regardless of if they look the same.

F: Yeah. They do. You still got that telescope?

A: I do.

F: Might take it out tomorrow night.

A: Are you sure?

F: Pfft, absolutely not. But I can't sit here and live in fear forever, can I?

A: Technically—

F: Don't answer that. Don't enable me.

A: I would never.

F: Uh-huh. Sure. You about ready to go in? I'm getting nervous again.

A: After you, my dear.

My sweet Alexandria,

Finch and I are going to sit outside tonight and stare up at the stars with my telescope. I cannot promise I will be able to share any offered information, so just know that I am taking care of him. He will be okay.

Love,
Aku

My Aku,

I hope it was lovely and enlightening. When are you going to propose?

Love,
Alexandria

My prying Alexandria,

I have, already. You know this. He will answer when and if he sees fit.

Love,
Aku

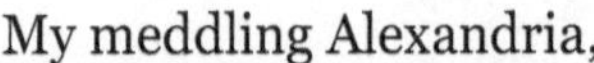

My silly little Aku,

You have been . . . less romantically inclined than I, so allow me to offer you some advice.

Humans do not see "I offer you eternity" as a proposal. Try instead, "Will you marry me?" And he was from the Neo-Social Era, correct? Get a ring.

Love,
Alexandria

My meddling Alexandria,

That's ridiculous. There is no more clear and overstated way to make my intentions known than to offer eternity together. That cannot be taken as anything *but* a romantic proposal. The women you have loved are beautiful and resplendent, but separate creatures from my Finch. He knows.

Love,
Aku

My stubborn Aku,

I will be blunt.

I do not think Finch wishes for eternity. He's already had his. This is where a proposal and a rebirth are separate: one is a promise of body, the other of heart and soul. You are currently asking for an entire future that he has no plans of ever seeing. Ask for the smaller infinity, my darling.

Love,
Alexandria

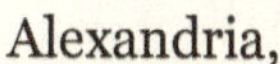

Alexandria,

I'm afraid you are mistaken. Finch hasn't decided on eternity yet; that does not *mean* he is refusing it. Finch is not choosing to die here. He just needs patience and time, as he always has, since the beginning.

Aku

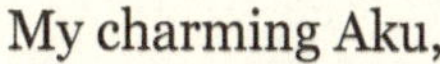

My charming Aku,

Do not be upset with me. If you are so very certain that Finch isn't quite done with this world, present him with the choice. The proposal, or the rebirth. Not an ultimatum; make sure he knows both offers will always be available. But just see. It is your job to protect this man. Go protect him.

Love, still,
Alexandria

My Alexandria,

We are engaged.

Love,
Aku

My beloved,

I am so sorry.

Love,
Alexandria

My Alexandria,

I will accept this for what it is. It is a good thing. Time might change his mind on the other. It must.

Love,
Aku

Sweet Aku,

Yes. Show him what it means to truly live. He is merely *surviving* right now. Teach him what a blessing watching the birds change hues can be.

Oh, Aku, my dear . . . show him the observatory.

Love,
Alexandria

[AUDIO TRANSCRIPTION]

Finch: So this is the infamous Finch Observatory, huh?

Aku: It was, yes. It seems the honeysuckle has taken over.

F: Yeah, it'll do that. Mm, still as sweet as I remember.

A: They're covering up the—hold on.

F: [whistles] Hey there, muscle man.

A: They're just vines.

F: More like tree trunks.

A: The honeysuckle—Ah. You are speaking of me, aren't you?

F: Yup.

A: You're ridiculous. There, now you can see.

F: Is that a . . .

A: A finch, yes. Alexandria painted it, long ago. I'm amazed it lasted.

F: It's beautiful.

A: It's you. Would you like to go inside?

F: And peer into deep space? Think I'm okay.

A: I will be right here beside you.

F: And I appreciate that. Ugh. Yeah, fine. Show me your little nerd cave or whatever.

A: *Our* nerd cave. I built this for you.

F: You're gonna make me all gushy inside.

A: You're human. You're *all* 'gushy' inside.

F: Like a Gushers, sure. Finch—Flavored fruit snack right here, bay-bee.

A: You are horrific. Here, help me open the apparatus?

F: Isn't that just jargon for thingamajig?

A: . . . perhaps.

F: Say it.

A: Say what?

F: Say thingamajig. Come on. It'll be funny.

A: [sigh] Will you please help me open the thingamajig?

F: Sure. Do I just grab these whozeewhatzits?

A: I'm enamored with you.

F: Thought I was horrific?

A: That too. Turn the wheel in tandem with me.

F: Shit, this thing is rusty.

A: Centuries will do that to a building. There. Clear views of the stars.

F: And horrors beyond our comprehension.

A: You have a clear view of me every night, my love.

F: You're not a horror.

A: Sure. Where would you like to look first? I have the location of most deep space objects memorized, plus a few I found on my own. We could see a far-off meteor shower if we're lucky.

F: Um, I . . . Can I see that?

A: Sure. It moves like this.

F: Thanks.

A: Where are you looking?

F: Um, here. You can look.

A: . . . Ah. I see.

F: There's nothing *to* see.

A: Of course not. You brought the Hephaestus back. What would be left?

F: I dunno, space debris? Metal? Bits of ship?

A: Horrors?

F: . . . yes.

A: My dear, I want you to look at me. I have scoured this entire night sky, every night, for millennia. From the moment you left Earth to the moment you returned. Whatever you saw out there, it has no interest in us now.

F: But—

A: Atticus, if it wanted you, it would have already taken you from me.

F: Okay.

A: Okay.

F: What's eternity like?

A: You ask me every night.

F: You have a new answer every night.

A: Look out to the stars. What do you feel?

F: . . . small. Small, and a bit scared, and a bit awed.

A: That is eternity.

F: You're not making a great case for yourself.

A: Shush. I'm not done.

F: Then please, continue.

A: Keep looking out to the stars.

F: I'm looking.

A: What do you feel?

F: Small, still and—Oh, okay, um, and you. Your hands.

A: Be more specific. No wonder your daily logs were always awful.

F: Hey! To be fair, I didn't give a shit about keeping up reports a-and—and uh . . .

A: The stars, Finch.

F: Right. Right. Stars. Um. I, I feel—heh, your lips on the back of my neck.

A: Mmhm.

F: A-and your hands on my waist.

A: Mmhm.

F: And your hands—Aku. *Aku*. What if someone comes in?

A: I own the place. Do you wish to feel eternity?

F: Yes.

A: Then allow me to show you.

[REST OF AUDIO CUT FOR DECENCY]

Tolstoy:

AAAAAAAAAAAAAAAAAAAAAAAAAAAAAAAAAAAAAAAAAAAAAAAAAA
AAAAAAAAAAAAAAAAAAAAAAAAAAAAAAAAAAAAAAAAAAAAAAAAAA
AAAAAAAAAAAAAAAAAAAAAAAAAAAAAAAAAAAAAAAAAAAAAAAAAA
AAAAAAAAAAAAAAAAAAAAAAAAAAAAAAAAAAAAAAAAAAAAAAAAAA
AAAAAAAAAAAAAAAAAAAAAAAAAAAAAAAAAAAAAAAAAAAAAAAAAA
AAAAAAAAAAAAAAAAAAAAAAAAAAAAAAAAAAAAAAAAAAAAAAAAAA
AAAAAAAAAAAAAAAAAAAAAAAAAAAAAAAAAAAAAAAAAAAAAAAAAA
AAAAAAAAAAAAAAAAAAAAAAAAAAAAAAAAAAAAAAAAAAAAAAAAAA
AAAAAAAAAAAAAAAAAAAAAAAAAAAAAAAAAAAAAAAAAAAAAAAAAA
AAAAAAAAAAAAAAAAAAAAAAAAAAAAAAAAAAAAAAAAAAAAAAAAAA
AAAAAAAAAAAAAAAAAAAAAAAAAAAAAAAAAAAAAAAAAAAAAAAAAA
AAAAAAAAAAAAAAAAAAAAAAAAAAAAAAAAAAA

               —Finch

My Alexandria,

  I took him to the observatory. It went very well. After spending some time inside, we walked around the grounds, looking at everything that became overgrown. There are still vegetables growing in the garden, though long cross-pollinated and mutated. We made good fun out of guessing what they once were.

Finch insisted on bringing a honeysuckle clipping back to Alaska, so when, next century, Alaska is covered in it, you know who to blame.

We looked at the birds living in the surrounding forest, and I took out my sketchbooks so we could compare. He saw the many attempts at his face and said nothing, though he ran his fingers across graphite cheeks. A few actually looked like him.

After studying plumage we took a foot trail down to the river. It is far deeper than last I was out there, and we stripped ourselves of our clothes and ran about in the cold water. Finch even crafted a fishing pole, and I am still mystified on *how*. The man is a marvel.

We made a fire and cooked the fish he caught, as well as roasting up some of the less-dubious vegetables. All in all, it was a good meal. We had no seasonings, and I was not permitted to fly to get some, so I intend to store a spice rack in my building soon. Some paprika would have blossomed our dish.

We talked more about the concept of eternity. It didn't seem to scare him so much, in the firelight. Less concern, more curiosity. It may bode well, but for now, I am going to be content with the flash of metal on his finger.

I hope your day was as good as mine.

Love,
Aku

[AUDIO TRANSCRIPTION]

Aku: My dear, tea is ready. Please, sit.

Finch: Can't.

A: Can't sit?

F: I'm going to burst at my seams, Aku.

A: Okay. Would pacing help?

F: No. Well—no, no. I just need to say this.

A: Rip the bandaid off.

F: I'm only gonna say this one time. Never again. Got it?

A: You . . . have my undivided attention.

F: Aliens isn't a good word.

A: . . . okay?

F: When the engine exploded and we spun into physics-breaking speed, everything outside was color and light. Everything. Okay so far?

A: Yes.

F: Mateo was with me. He was trying to get the ship back online. Meredith was in the room that exploded and she was drifting. Out there. In space. Only, she wasn't inside out. Her guts didn't come out her mouth, y'know, she was okay. With me?

A: I'm with you.

F: Okay. It's—it—

A: I'm here.

F: I know. It—I can't—describe it. I can't describe it. It *hurts* to think about, okay?

A: It can wait. If it isn't the right time.

F: No that's the thing it *can't*—if I stop now I'll never say it. It—you know the, the whispering?

A: Yes.

F: That.

A: That?

F: That. Aku—

A: Hey. I'm here. You're shaking. Finch—

F: Aliens is a *bad word* because it doesn't *cover it*. I watched it—I don't know what it *did* to her, Aku, but it—she was—torn. Torn? And I . . . heard her.

A: She . . . I don't understand.

F: I heard it in my head, our heads, everyone's—like we were all suddenly *connected*. The screaming, the—the *whispering*—Aku—

A: Babe—

F: It *took her*. And then it—did it crawl? I can't—do you know?

A: No. I don't.

F: I don't either. It doesn't *make sense* and the words don't *work*. They're not enough. A—a million fucking languages and not a goddamn correct word!

A: Then tell me poorly. Use the wrong words.

F: It crawled to us. It—ate? It ate. It consumed. It destroyed—Mateo, then Chloe, and Ashraf, and Todd, and—

A: And not you.

F: And not me.

A: Why . . . not you?

F: I—I don't know. I think it did. It tried? There are missing pieces, in my head. Moments of just—just *panic* surrounded by nothingness and then—and then sometimes—sometimes you. Sometimes I saw you. Does that . . . make sense?

A: No, but I am following.

F: I saw you . . . here? Probably here. Like a dream. I think I was dreaming, or *it* was dreaming, I don't know, but I remember a sound like—like an alarm, in my hearing aids. That stupid loud *obnoxious* noise that means the . . . the battery is dying.

A: I'm with you. I'm here.

F: And I think it startled it, maybe? Enough? Or maybe it let me go for some reason, I don't—I was back in the ship. And it was there, crawling, eyes on me and I didn't know what to do so I turned the sensitivity up until it was nothing but screeching fucking feedback, and I closed my eyes and screamed and then it was just . . . gone. And you were there telling me I was alive.

A: And you haven't seen it since?

F: In my dreams. Watching me. I don't know why, but I know it's—real. The dreams. It's watching me. Even now. I still hear them.

A: My love—

F: Mateo and Ashraf and Chloe and Meredith and Todd in my—in my head if I'm—if things are too quiet or I'm dreaming or—they're just . . .

A: Screaming?

F: Yes. It's going to eat us too, you know. It's going to be the end. The last things we will ever know will be sharp teeth and *whispers*.

A: You don't know that.

F: How could I not? I was in it. I know. I *know*. And we are standing here in Alaska like it isn't *out there*. Like it isn't *watching me. Crawling for me.*

A: It's been there this whole time.

F: It has.

A: It's read everything we've ever sent.

F: Probably.

A: Then, to me, that says nothing has changed.

F: How can you say that? *Everything has changed!*

A: Has it? Can you do anything to stop it?

F: I—

A: Can you even slow it down?

F: No, I—

A: Can you predict it?

F: No. No.

A: Then we do what humans have always been good at doing: we *ignore death*. We pretend it isn't out there. We hold each other when we have nightmares. We fill up your head with love and poetry and music. I already told you, my love, we are here until we aren't, just like everyone else.

F: How can you be so—so *nonchalant?*

A: The other option is to hide forever, and I have spent too many nights begging for you. I cannot. I ignore it. So it goes.

F: But what if—if we get eaten? If we *die?*

A: I don't think that's an if. I don't think that's ever been an *if.*

F: What do I do? How do I forget it?

A: Do you trust me?

F: Yes.

A: Time. You give it time. Humans always forget the horrors. I should know.

F: I don't have enough time to forget that.

A: I know.

F: Could you promise I would forget it? If I had enough time?

A: I wish to say yes, but no. I can't. I couldn't forget you, even if I tried to.

F: So if I never forget . . . ?

A: I will still be here, regardless.

F: And if it shows up in the sky in a million years?

A: I'll hold your hand. You will not face it alone.

F: You can't fight it.

A: No. I can't. But I'll hold your hand and face it regardless.

F: Okay. Okay.

A: Can you breathe now?

F: Bit better, yeah. Can we go inside? I can hear them again.

A: Of course.

My dearest Alexandria,

Life goes on. Finch has said all he is going to say. He doesn't close the curtains anymore. He wakes with a smile sometimes. He asks about eternity daily. He's learning Rhonik. He's cemented himself, if not somewhat loosely, back into the flow of time, and I think it's good for him. I only hope we are lucky enough to get enough years to make up for all the lost ones.

Visit soon.

Love,
Aku

[AUDIO TRANSCRIPTION]

Aku: Your tomatoes are doing nicely.

Finch: They are, aren't they? BLTs for lunch?

A: That sounds lovely.

F: You've got that look again.

A: What look?

F: Like you're thinking better of something.

A: I am.

F: Out with it, or I'll have to kiss it from you.

A: Well, now I don't want to say a word.

F: Cheeky.

A: Eternity.

F: Ah.

A: I apologize. I shouldn't have brought it up.

F: Hmm . . . Will you make bread tonight? I'm still bad at it.

A: Yes, my love. Anything for you.

F: Well, then. I suppose it's only fair if I give you an answer.

A: Only if you're sure.

F: You know, I sent so many cries for help.

A: I know.

F: I fought for the ship back.

A: I know.

F: Do you know why?

A: Survival. It's what humans do best.

F: You're being highly unromantic right now while I'm trying so very hard to be romantic.

A: Sorry. I'm actually very nervous. Why did you keep fighting?

F: Because you were waiting here for me.

A: Finch . . .

F: I've decided. I want eternity with you. Not with every other atom in the universe, Aku, but with *you*. I know how this ends. I want every second I can get. I want to hold your hand at the end.

A: Are you saying what I think you're—

F: You. Me. Eternity. Every weird vegetable. Every lost acronym. I want it with you. If the universe wants me, it'll have to come here and get me itself. Deal?

A: Deal. My beloved, my sweet Finch, of *course* it's a deal.

F: Okay. I'm never speaking of this again, so if you have any more questions, ask them *now*.

A: Only one. Do you regret the mission? Knowing how it ends?

F: What ending? Eternity with my stupid penpal? Never in a million years.

A: You might see it, you know. A million years.

F: Good. I'll need something new to write about.

A: I love you. You know that, I'm aware, but I need to reiterate it, here and now. I love you.

F: I love you, too. Now are you going to feed me or will I have to seduce you again?

A: I mean, I was absolutely going to, but let's try this seduction route, see where it leads.

F: You're terrible.

A: At this? Nice try. I'm very good at this.

F: Prove it. Let's dance.

A: Why, you cheeky little—

Alexandria:

Thanks for the teacups :)

Love,
Atticus

acknowledgements

I'd be remiss not to send thanks to Galileo, Copernicus, Kepler, and Messier, for looking to the heavens and longing to explore them; to Holly, for yelling at me in my Discord DMs; to Amy, for yelling at me in my text messages; to Jess, for general world-building extraordinaire-ness; to Ari, who I met ages ago in the stars; to Molly, for being the same sort of strange as me; and to Ricky, for sitting beside my telescope with me on mosquito-ridden nights.

A thousand miles an hour, every one of us. Race you there.

about the contributors

Rascal Hartley is a speculative fiction author. When they aren't staring at the night sky or painting sea storms, you can find them reading books to their dog or being a general nuisance.

Carly A-F is a freelance illustrator from the UK making colourful, dramatic art inspired by nature, science, myth and magic. Her work is a combination of digital colour and traditional media; she illustrates for a wide variety of projects including book covers, posters, TTRPGs, and picture books.

Matt Blairstone (he/him) is a writer, editor, artist, indie comics creator and the publisher/founder of **Tenebrous Press**. He lives in Portland, Oregon. Ghosts believe in him.

Grab another Tenebrous title!

Grab another
Tenebrous title!

Home of New Weird Horror, New Weird Dark
Fiction, Oddities, Abnormalities and All Manner
of Eccentricities You Never Knew You Needed
More Than Oxygen

FIND OUT MORE:

www.tenebrouspress.com

@TenebrousPress on social media

HAIL THE TENEBROUS CULT

www.ingramcontent.com/pod-product-compliance
Lightning Source LLC
Chambersburg PA
CBHW031540310726
48971CB00008B/2566